Fire

Demon

Dawn

Fire
Demon
Dawn

Alfred Wurr

For my readers.

Contents

Welcome

Thank you very much for your purchase of *Fire Demon Dawn*, a stand-alone side story to my first-in-series novel, *Phantom Frost*. Written in Canadian English (as all my books are) and told from the perspective of Bodhi Institute Security Director Harland Dixon, it tells of the events that occurred at the covert facility in parallel with Shivurr's adventures.

When you are done reading *Fire Demon Dawn*, if you'd like to read *Phantom Frost*, you can find links to purchase it at alfredwurr.com—as well as subsequent books in the series as they become available.

Either way, I hope you enjoy finding out more about the Bodhi Institute, its denizens, and the forces and perils of Shivurr's universe within the pages of this book. I've certainly enjoyed escaping back to the '80s during the "uncertain times" in which I've written it.

Fire
Demon
Dawn

Chapter 1

Moths to Flame

Acrid smoke tickled Harland's nose as he approached the still-smoking attack helicopter. Metal groaned as the aircraft's burned-out husk teetered in the wind. The twisted rotor swivelled. The flames were out, the once powerful and expensive machine a blackened lump of useless metal, illuminated by only the light of the Milky Way and the sliver of the waxing crescent moon. He'd not seen a downed bird since Vietnam.

Most of the tents used by the scientists studying the dais were gone or little more than scorched tatters of fabric, but two had survived the assault. A third tent rose from the desert floor, erected by a group of men, a hundred feet away, using the headlights of the trucks they had arrived on as a makeshift light source. Others strung wiring and placed light stands, preparing more suitable illumination for those responsible for analyzing recent events.

Harland slipped off his blazer and draped it over an arm. Despite the late hour, warm air drew sweat from his brow, but it evaporated before it could accumulate and run down his face. He didn't mind. Heat and aridity soothed the aches and pains that he had acquired in decades of serving his country. The former were in fact the perks that had compelled him to accept the Bodhi Institute posting many years ago. He'd take them over the winters of his childhood any day of the week.

His tenure with the CIA had made him an ideal candidate to head security at the Bodhi Group's Nevada facility, and he was proud to be a part of it. To contribute to its cause. To protect his country and the principles of liberty and equality upon which it had been founded. To work with the Group's other member nations who likewise sought to preserve their own way of life, by cooperating in scientific endeavours that would keep the West ahead of the bad guys.

As his counterpart, Bodhi Institute Executive Director Jeffrey Wallace, PhD, had often told him, you don't get ahead of everyone else by thinking conventionally. Knowing that, the Group didn't merely try to get to the next logical step in technological development first. The other guys would always be right behind; adjacent scientific advancements become inevitable once the foundation is there. If someone invents the wheel, attaching it to a box to make a wagon isn't going to be far behind.

The Group's founders knew that the best way to get so far ahead of the other guys that they'd have no hope of catching up was to go after the non-obvious. To be the only one in the race, because the other guys don't even know the racetrack exists. Backed by prodigious funding from a host of nations, they favoured research and development projects that explored the strange and bizarre, investigating unlikely, unconventional and even ridiculous avenues of study, even those dismissed by the scientific community at large. All in the hope of finding something completely new and revolutionary.

And the boldness had paid off more than once, leading to discoveries that were shared or loaned to associated agencies, even his former employer, the CIA. The distribution of that knowledge, even to a friendly government agency, had to be handled with great care, however. Staying ahead, even in a cold war, meant *keeping* secrets. Even the existence of discoveries had to be protected against theft. Thieves prefer to burgle houses that they *know* have something worth stealing. Plus, secrecy made it easier to pursue the research without worrying about public perception or the ridicule of the larger scientific community.

So they needed more than just scientists and engineers. They needed people like Harland. Those who knew how to keep secrets and how to protect them. And, perhaps more importantly, those who would stand ready to protect the Group *from* some secrets that should have stayed buried.

A rhythmic thumping rose over the wind and cicadas. The security director watched as an airborne helicopter approached low over the desert before setting down on the landing zone a few hundred feet away. The doors opened, and several people spilled forth and began unloading cases and equipment onto the desert floor.

The new arrivals made for one of the field tents. After a few steps, one of their number broke away from the larger group. He strode toward a couple of Harland's security agents, one of several pairs Harland had stationed around the area to provide overwatch against attack. The shorter of the two, Jesus Jimenez, an early-thirties field agent, held up a hand as the man approached.

As Jimenez's flashlight lit the newcomer's face, Harland recognized him from photos he'd seen. He was a recent transfer from one of the Bodhi Group's northern facilities, a scientist with a PhD in chemistry, if he remembered correctly. As security director, he made a point of reviewing the personnel files of those transferring in, but he had yet to meet the man in person—it had been a busy week.

Jimenez tilted his head in Harland's direction. His lips moved, but his words faded in the wind. Both agents smirked at the new arrival's back for several heartbeats as he shambled over, then back to their desert surroundings.

"Uh, hi. I'm Gary," the man said. "Gary Ashdon." He brushed the sleeve of his white lab coat across his brow and extended a hand. "I'm new on Project Sky Fire. Are you Harley?"

The security director's chin sank into his neck. "Do I look like I ride a motorcycle?"

"I…I'm sorry?"

"My name's not *Harley.*"

"Of course. Harland. I meant no—"

"Are we friends?"

"Uh…no."

Harland popped an eyebrow and stared.

Ashdon squinted, dropping the hand Harland had failed to take back to his side. He stole a look over his shoulder at Jimenez and Carmichael. The two agents burst into laughter and waved. Jimenez's snow-white teeth shone in the starlight as he slapped his colleague's back and gave Harland a thumbs-up. The security director's lips quivered, then stilled.

Ashdon swung back to face him and pushed his glasses up the bridge of his nose. "No…sir?"

Harland nodded. "Better. That or Director or Mr. Dixon will do nicely."

Ashdon straightened. "Uh…understood. Sorry, Director…*sir.*"

"Don't sweat it, Ashdon," Harland said, chuckling at last and slapping the smaller man on the shoulder. "I'm just messing with you."

"Oh, I see," Ashdon said. He smiled like someone learning how to do it for the first time. "Funny."

"Got to give the new guy a hard time. Either Dixon or Harland is good. But seriously, don't ever call me *Harley* again. Got it?"

"Understood," Ashdon replied. "The agents…well…I meant no disrespect."

Harland shrugged. "Why are you here?"

"Dr. Huggins has tasked the team with finding additional entity remains."

Harland cocked an eyebrow. "And you're not doing that because?"

"I understand you witnessed the tail end of the battle." Ashdon looked around. "If you could provide an estimate of enemy numbers, we'll know how many crystals are likely to be in the vicinity."

"Smart thinking," Harland said. "Not just book smart, I see."

"Thank you, sir," Ashdon said, beaming. "I was also hoping you could describe the events you witnessed." He waved a hand at the desert expanse. "If so, we may be able to focus our search on more likely locations as well."

Harland shook his head. "Too dark to see much now. You boys will be better off waiting until morning. You should be able to follow the scorch trails these things leave in their wakes to where they fell."

"Nonetheless," Ashdon said, "it is advisable to have as much intelligence as possible. If it rains or the wind erodes the trails by morning—"

"This is a desert, Ashdon; not likely to rain anytime soon…but your point still stands." Harland extended an arm. "Our men dropped a half dozen a few hundred yards that way—before they reached the camp. The enemy corpses still smouldered when we arrived." He snapped on a flashlight and aimed the beam into the desert. "The surviving entities were engaging our men over there, there, and…there."

Ashdon bugged his eyes and swallowed. "That must

have been terrifying."

"No doubt," Harland said. "Have you seen them yet? We've got a few at the Institute now."

The corners of Ashdon's mouth dipped as he studied the desert. "I don't have clearance to go that deep."

"I didn't ask about your personal life," Harland said with a lopsided grin.

"Huh?"

Harland sighed. *Eggheads. No sense of humour.* "Never mind. Harriet submitted a request earlier today. I guess she hasn't told you."

Ashdon brightened. "That's great news. I'm eager to see them up close. They sound quite fascinating."

"Yeah, right," Harland said. "Maybe from a place of safety." He pointed a thumb at the helicopter. "Except, even when you *think* you're safe, things can change fast."

Ashdon ambled toward the ruin. "Is it true they're pure fire?"

"Not quite," Harland said. "Flames engulf them, but their bodies have substance. Their cores are vaguely humanoid." He moved his hands sinuously as if tracing the outline of an invisible form. "It's as if they're sculpted of molten rock, viscous liquid flowing and bubbling, yet, impossibly, holding shape." He scowled. "At least until you put enough ordnance into them. Spill enough of it, they eventually fall and die."

"Then they're alive?" Ashdon breathed, holding out a hand toward the fallen chopper as if testing for residual warmth.

"I don't know how anything like that could be alive or have evolved but, yes, looks that way. Some say they're of…supernatural origin. Others think they're alien invaders. One thing's for sure…they're not from around here."

"Unbelievable," Ashdon said. "Your men deserve medals. To dare to stand in the path of such fearsome creatures. Their courage…it's…impressive."

Harland nodded. "To their credit, they fell back in an orderly fashion." He scanned the desert, reliving the scene. "If they'd run, they'd all be dead now, I suspect. These things move *fast*. You run from them, you're likely to die tired. As it is, we still lost too many." He grimaced. "*One* is too many."

Ashdon studied his feet. "I'm sorry, sir."

Harland waved a hand. "Not your fault. My men are well-paid patriots. This is what they signed up for." He looked Ashdon in the eyes. "And Dixon is fine…seriously."

"Yes, sir."

Harland snorted. "Now you're just messing with *me*. Anything else I can help with?"

"We've also been directed to look for other artifacts—like the platform being studied here."

"Doubt you'll find any," Harland said. "We haven't found any closer to each other than several miles. Doesn't seem to be rhyme or reason to their positioning. Some were buried under soil, too."

"Is that the dais?" Ashdon pointed toward the centre of the camp, where men wielding liquid nitrogen canisters sprayed the desert floor as a tractor crawled into position. "The one that they were examining."

"For now," Harland said. "We're moving it—and the others—back to the facility, in case there are more incursions. It's too exposed out here, especially with those creatures manifesting out of thin air."

Ashdon blinked. "You think more will come?"

"That's the general consensus," Harland said. "They seem drawn to the platforms like moths to flame. Except, far as we know, they don't need line of sight to find them."

"If that's true, we might be able to—"

"One of you Dixon?" said a man wearing a flight suit and helmet as he ran over.

Harland bobbed his head.

"Langford said you're needed back at the Institute."

Harland tilted his head back and regarded the tip of his nose through narrowed eyes. "She say why?"

"Something about a lead on…*Winterboy*," said the pilot with a grin. He shrugged. "She said you'd know what that meant."

Harland winced. *Just because it's a code name doesn't mean she should be tossing it around.* "Forget you heard that name."

"Already forgotten," the pilot said with a two-fingered salute. He thrust a thumb over his shoulder. "I'm to fly you back the moment you're ready. Do you need more time here? I'll shut down if you do. Save fuel for the return flight."

Harland looked at Ashdon. "We good?"

Ashdon scanned the area and nodded. "We should be able to take it from here." He extended a hand, which Harland shook. "I appreciate your time, sir. You've been a big help."

"Dixon."

"Yes, of course…Dixon."

"Good man." Harland pointed a finger at Ashdon for as long as it took him to wink. "I'll see you back at the Institute." He turned toward the pilot. "Let's move."

Chapter 2

Necessary Evil

Harland leaped from the helicopter onto the roof of the Nevada Bodhi Institute. He straightened his blazer and strode over to Cynthia Langford. The smartly dressed forty-something woman awaited his arrival with a sombre expression on her face. Pretty and petite; Harland towered over her as they shook hands; even in heels, the top of her head reached only his chin.

They exchanged brief pleasantries, then entered a waiting elevator. His companion pressed a button and the doors closed, shutting out the cacophonous racket of chopping rotor blades. A moment later, his stomach raced to catch up as the elevator car dropped, heading for the depths of the mostly subterranean facility.

Normally he'd be meeting with Bodhi Institute Executive Director Jeffrey Wallace, PhD: his administrative counterpart and frequent pain in the ass. While Harland held dominion over Institute security, Wallace managed all else. As such, the two often needed to confer, particularly in times of crisis and high alert.

As Dr. Wallace's assistant, Langford often acted as his proxy when the Institute's administrative head was indisposed or otherwise engaged. Problems arose at all hours in an international organization like the Bodhi Group, and relying on Cynthia ensured that Wallace got his beauty sleep. She had strict instructions during such times to wake her boss only in an emergency.

Finally able to speak without shouting secrets into the desert air, Harland asked, "What's this about a lead on Winterboy?"

"We may have caught a break searching employee homes," Cynthia said, stifling a yawn. With the recent crises, Harland knew that she had also been pulling all-nighters, assisting Wallace during daylight hours, and liaising with Harland and his team throughout the night. "Two of our agents missed a check-in earlier tonight. They were conducting surprise searches of employee homes, as you ordered."

"Maybe they're not near a phone," Harland said. "Could be car trouble. It wouldn't be the first time."

"Well," Cynthia said, "they'd been out of touch too long for that, so we sent a team to check the next house on their list."

Harland nodded. "Good call. Whose place?"

She cleared her throat. "Uh…Scott Green's."

"Huh…and where does Green live?"

"Las Vegas. On the west side of town."

Harland leaned against the wall to face her. *This could be bad.* He knew the computer systems administrator and programmer well. When it came to information technology, Scott was his go-to guy. He sighed, propping his elbow with one arm and stroking the stubble on his chin with the other. "What did they find?"

"No sign of our agents," she replied, "but their company car was being towed from Green's driveway. Apparently it was a burned-out wreck. And the squad noticed fire damage to other houses on the street."

Harland's jaw dropped. "*Another* incursion?"

She smiled, but it didn't reach her eyes. "It seems likely, judging by the damage." She leaned against the wall opposite him, resting her bottom on the steel guardrail that bordered the car. "They thought they saw what looked like scorch trails in the street, but it was dark. Our people didn't witness the attack or speak to any neighbours, so we're not yet absolutely certain."

"Check nearby hospitals," Harland said. "See if our agents were admitted."

"Already did," Cynthia replied. "They're in the ICU, being treated for burns and other injuries."

"Which agents?"

"McGregor and Grant."

"And what about Shiv—Winterboy? Was he there?"

"There was no sign of him either."

"And Scott?"

"Nope."

Harland pinched the bridge of his nose. "I'm failing to see how this is a lead on Winterboy. Another entity attack is definitely worth investigation, but we still don't know if there's a link between them and our snowy friend. The footage from the chamber was too poor."

"They found a van parked in Green's driveway."

"Like the one from Tonopah?"

"Exactly," Cynthia said with a nod. "The plates match too."

"Well…that *is* interesting," Harland said. "I suppose he might know them. It could just be a coincidence that they ended up there."

"The probability of *that* seems low," Cynthia replied. "Occam's Razor—"

"Was there any sign of the passengers?"

Cynthia smiled. "They were inside the house. Our team's bringing them here for questioning."

"Well done," Harland said. "When do they arrive?"

She checked her watch. "Thirty to forty minutes…if

they're keeping to the speed limit."

"Very good," Harland said. "Put them in one of the conference rooms on the second floor when they do, and let me know when they're secure."

"Of course."

"Oh," Harland said, snapping his fingers. "Make sure we've got a few bugs planted. I want to hear what they say to each other."

Cynthia furrowed her brow.

"What's on your mind?" Harland asked.

He pushed off the wall and squared off with the doors as they slid aside with a ding. He held back, motioning Cynthia to precede him with an after-you gesture.

Exiting, she turned to face him. "Where are we going? To your office?"

"Yeah," he said, striding ahead. "Anyway, you were saying."

"Well," she began, "I know you like him…but…it's hard to imagine that Scott isn't also involved. The unavoidable conclusion is that…*he's* the one that helped Subject Winterboy escape."

"Let's not be too hasty. Scott's no commie." Like everyone else, Scott had been thoroughly vetted before coming to work at the Institute. Born and raised in the good old USA by a family that had immigrated to the country generations ago, he was as unlikely to be a Soviet agent as anyone Harland could think of. There was always the chance he'd been compromised—blackmailed into acting on their behalf—but if the kid had skeletons in his closet that could be used against him, the Group would surely have uncovered them when screening him. And that presupposed that the Soviets were involved in the escape. If they weren't involved, that left Scott helping Shivurr simply out of sympathy. He had had little contact with the guy, though, so why would he risk helping him? Sure, the new intel meant that he'd have to be investigated more deeply, but Harland wasn't ready to convict him just yet. "Someone might be trying to set him up as a patsy. Maybe Winterboy got Scott's address from whoever helped him. They might have shown up there to cast suspicion on him, and off the real culprit."

Cynthia looked doubtful. "I think you may be grasping—"

Harland held up a hand. "I agree," he said. "It doesn't look good, but we need to be sure. We need to talk to McGregor and Grant. Find out what they know."

"They're keeping them sedated," she said from several steps behind him. He slowed his pace, allowing her to catch up. "For the pain. We won't be talking to them for a while. That is, if they survive."

"That bad?"

Her forehead crinkled. "I'm afraid so."

"All right," Harland said. "Set up an interview schedule for everyone in Scott's group. If he's involved, we need to know for sure."

"You just finished talking to everyone the other day."

They arrived at the door to Harland's office. He jingled his keys and turned to face her.

"And came up empty. If Scott is involved, someone that he works with might be in cahoots with him or know something. Either way, I'll need them to look for any clues left behind, physical *and* digital. He can't have covered his tracks *that* well."

"I'll get right on it."

"Thanks." Harland winked. "Well done, Langford—grabbing the kids."

"Thank you," Cynthia said. "I was worried you'd think we'd overstepped."

"How's that?"

"They're American citizens," she said, biting her cheek. "We're not a law enforcement agency. Technically—"

Harland waved a hand. "Finding Winterboy is more important than ever. I've got a feeling he's the key to stopping the fire entity attacks. Don't look so worried. Wallace will square things, if it comes to that."

"But nabbing citizens off the streets…it's…"

"What? *Fascist?*"

Cynthia nodded.

She was right. They *were* Americans, and that *meant* something, but sometimes you had to drift across legal lines to get things done. If the kids had to endure a little inconvenience to help protect their country, it wasn't a lot to ask.

"Look, Langford." Harland put a hand on her shoulder. "This country isn't perfect, but it's the best this world's ever seen. Better than the Greeks. Better than the Romans too. But barbarians are at the gates. Some are already inside. So we've got to do whatever it takes to defend ourselves against them." He lowered his voice to a whisper. "Maybe grabbing them isn't *strictly* legal, but it was necessary. Sometimes sacrifices must be made."

"But they've been studying Winterboy for years, and they still know *so* little…"

"Oh, they've figured out a bit." Harland turned to unlock the door. "Someday, maybe it'll be enough to give us an edge over the bad guys. Even if they don't yet understand the whys, you don't need to know why gravity works to use a catapult." He pushed the door open and turned to face her. "Besides, I'm more interested in what he might be able to tell us about this new enemy. He was at the chamber when these things first arrived. I know it in my guts. The camera footage was pretty lousy, but I asked the techs to try to enhance a section that *might* be him."

Cynthia's eyes widened. "With his memory loss, what could he tell us that would help?"

"What is lost can be found," Harland said. "Besides, what better to fight fire with than frost?"

"Right," she said, smirking. "There is a certain symmetry to it."

"That's the spirit." He gave her an attaboy nudge on the shoulder and tilted his head toward the open door. "Now…if you'll excuse me…"

"Of course, Harland," she said, turning to leave.

He slipped inside, kicking a stack of letters that had been dropped through the mail slot across the floor as he did so. He stooped to collect them and shut the door. Thumbing through them, he made his way to a desk cluttered with personnel files, detritus of his investigation into Shivurr's disappearance. He moved them aside and grabbed a letter opener.

He spent the next half hour reading correspondence, eventually getting to a thin legal-sized manila envelope containing a large, glossy black-and-white photograph. The photograph appeared to be a still of the Great Basin Desert chamber that the Bodhi Group had been studying now for many years. An unsolved enigma, it held sculptures, artwork, and architectural elements characteristic of Ancient Greece and Rome: artifacts that had no business existing in Nevada. Even more unlikely, it contained crystals, great and small, that crackled with unknown energy, and a dais with a glowing ball of roiling frost that had enraptured Bodhi Group scientists for years now.

He had visited the chamber a number of times in the past, and it still filled him with awe, but the writing on the photograph was what drew his eye. A red marker had been used to circle a portion in the lower-right corner of the grainy image. The letters WB had been drawn in the margin with an arrow pointing to the circle.

Harland pulled a magnifying glass from a drawer of his desk and scrutinized the predominantly white contents of the red circle.

"Son of a bitch," he said, smiling and slapping his free hand on the desk. "There you are."

Chapter 3

Winterboy

It was him. Shivurr, code name Winterboy. Thick fog had filled the chamber at the time of the photo's capture, making him easy to miss. Only enlargement and enhancement of the image allowed Harland to discern the outline of Shivurr's form—enough to confirm that the snowman had been on the scene.

In his mind's eye, he could see Shivurr with perfect clarity. He probably always would. An impossible creature out of myth, walking and talking, would do that. A wonder to behold, so much *more* than a mere *snowman*.

As one might expect, at his core, he was three spheres, stacked atop each other, each a little smaller as they rose. The lab boys had concluded the shape to be the most conducive to channelling the energies at Shivurr's command while also providing structural strength.

His face was more expressive and detailed than a child's snowman, though perhaps less than a human being's.

Well, that or the expressive subtleties are just too hard to discern within the icy blues and whites of Shivurr's face.

And there were no stick arms for this snow being either. Instead, his arms were elongated, thick, with rounded biceps and strong hands with long fingers ending in sharp nails of icelike spikes. Hands capable of fine motor control; he could be a painter or predator.

He'd be frightening except for the friendly expression,

easy wide smile, and sparkling blue eyes that looked upon the world with perpetual wonder. No eyes of coal for this guy, and no carrot nose either. Pointed, sure, but a bit more rounded at the end and solid ice-white like the rest of him. His *skin*, if you could call it that, was just a solid layer of gleaming ice. It somehow shifted and undulated with his every move, malleable like snakeskin while still impermeable to outside contaminants.

He had no legs, though; just feet that moved along the circumference of the bottom sphere. In truth, as Harland knew from Shivurr's files, his legs lay within the lower sphere. His feet were attached to ice crystal bones, bones that articulated within the solid mass. They moved through the snow, somehow, as if through liquid or air, moving his feet front to back, giving an impression more of gliding over the earth than walking upon it.

Perhaps most remarkable was his melodic voice and talent for mimicry that he used to speak with an accent that was an amalgam of those around him. When you heard him speak and argued with him, you quickly saw the intellect and character that occupied this impossible unlikeliest of forms.

It makes no sense that he should exist, but does anything *existing make sense, or does it only seem to because we are* accustomed *to it? So, yeah, Shivurr is like a* snowman *the way a human resembles a Muppet. He's the real deal come to life; the other a crude approximation, accurate in the broad details but resembling Shivurr no closer than a child's teddy resembles a grizzly bear.*

Despite that, someone thought it would be funny to give him a scarf to make him look that much more like a child's snowman. Whether Shivurr thought it meant as a joke or not, he wore it anyway.

For all Harland knew, the gift *might* have been sincere. Shivurr had a way of disarming people. They tended to trust him instinctively for some reason.

Harland envied that. He tended to rub people the wrong way. His good-natured jokes were often mistaken for hostility. *Touchy pricks.*

Though he doubted Shivurr returned the sentiment, he admired and liked the guy, even if he wasn't human. He didn't enjoy being his jailer, but as the Brits liked to say, needs must.

Keeping the flame of liberty burning requires sacrifices. The hippie bastards that had campaigned against the Vietnam War hadn't understood that, hadn't seen the long game being played by the Reds. That was the deception inherent in the Cold War, where the danger was vague, not easily attributed to the true source.

Vietnam wasn't like Dad's war, he thought, *when the enemy was clear and unambiguous.* Those that had fought in the world wars had had the entire country at their backs, and those that had returned had done so to a hero's welcome.

Not so for Harland's war.

Though he had left early to join the Group, where he felt he could do more to protect the country he loved, he sympathized with the soldiers who'd died over there, unsupported and reviled by half the country. As a former CIA agent operating from the shadows, Harland accepted that risking life and limb without recognition came with the job, but a *little* gratitude for those running into hails of bullets would be nice.

Whatever. If he had to be the bad guy to save them, then so be it. At least the president got it. He'd had his doubts about a former actor as president, but Reagan understood that freedom had to be fought for every single day, that you needed to give people a hand up, not a handout, and that indulging the lazy and deviant only emboldened them to take more, to engage in more aberrant behaviour.

So at the end of the day, it didn't matter if he'd be judged unkindly by well-meaning and naive bleeding hearts for the actions he took to keep on protecting them. Like other patriots before him, he'd make whatever sacrifice was required to defend his country and its way of life. He'd sooner die than live unfree and had a seething hatred for those that would willingly submit to a loss of freedom for the illusion of safety, or to appease evil.

He just tried not to think too hard about the contradiction in taking Shivurr's freedom to protect his own. It was the guilt he felt over doing so that had made him do what he could to make the snowman's stay as pleasant as possible. Games, soda pop, movies, computer access, and a comfortable (for him) room, Harland, in consultation with Wallace, had allowed him most everything he'd wanted.

He didn't get the appeal of half the things Shivurr requested. Movies, sure (depending on the genre), but arcade games? He had no time for such things. What little downtime he had these days involved poker, drinking scotch—maybe a cigar or two.

He had told himself that keeping Shivurr here was in his best interests. *Where would an ice creature like him go anyway?* He'd melt and die for sure out in the world. Given that they were saving his life, it seemed only fair that he should give *something* back. If that meant the occasional experimental discomfort, it had to be better than dying of exposure. He had tried to explain it to Shivurr; tried to make him understand why it had to be this way, but he never seemed to get it.

Then again, Harland's assumptions about Shivurr's fragility had so far proven to be wrong. It should have meant certain death, but somehow, he'd survived and eluded them for almost a week now in the dry heat of the Nevada summer.

Tough guy. The trials that the Group had put him through proved that, but his desert odyssey showed even more impressive resilience. *But why'd he take such a risk?*

He looked at the photograph again. It turned out that the guy did have somewhere to go after all. In retrospect, it made sense that he would return to the chamber where he had first arrived.

He must be trying to get home.

Angry as he felt to lose him, he respected Shivurr's desire to be free and return home. He took a deep breath and tried to forget for the moment that he had every one of his agents working to ensure that that would not happen.

What Harland didn't know was if or how Shivurr was connected to the fire creatures. They both came from the same chamber but were otherwise polar opposites.

Harland still hadn't ruled out the possibility that these creatures had been developed in a Soviet lab, but a connection to Shivurr seemed more likely. They were first spotted at the chamber where he'd arrived, and there were the things the snowman had said in the past. Shivurr hadn't spoken English when he'd first arrived, but he'd learned quickly. Once he'd known how, he'd warned of an imminent disaster being brought on the world by the industries of humankind, and the gestures and diagrams that he kept drawing had abruptly made sense.

"Too hot," he had said. "The world has been too hot for too long. We must restore all frost or the earth is doomed."

You would expect as much from a snowman—wanting to make the world *all frost*—so no one took him too seriously. Sure, some scientists had been talking about a greenhouse effect warming the planet—*something to do with carbon dioxide*—but few paid much attention to them either. *What difference does a few degrees make, and how can you even tell with certainty? The world's a big place.* Besides, having been raised in the north of the country, Harland liked the sound of warmer winters. More likely, any warming was simply a part of the planet's natural cycle, or so some Bodhi Group scientists had suggested at the time. Admittedly, the subject lay outside their fields, but they were *smart* people.

In spite of those assurances, these fire entities had Harland questioning whether the snowman might not have been right. A colder and snowier world *would* be far less attractive to life forms composed of fire and magma (or whatever they were made of). Even so, an ice age would also be disastrous for warm-blooded human beings. That left humanity trapped between fire and ice. It also meant that the Group wasn't about to help bring such a thing about, even if it were possible to do so.

They needed to talk to Shivurr about these things. More appeared at each incursion, and they didn't go down easy. If they were to reach a populated area, the deaths would be catastrophic. The panic they'd cause would likely lead to even more deaths. Humanity wasn't ready for such revelations. No, they needed to stop them at their source. *Whatever, wherever that source is…before it gets totally out of hand.*

While he might no longer recall the creatures, the missing pieces of his mind could be restored; so said the researchers that had studied him. Most of what they'd taken from him lay secure, many floors below, in an archival vault freezer. Efforts were already underway to recover those sent to other facilities, in case they were needed, as well. The science teams couldn't be sure as they had only a vague sense of which memories lay in which samples, and some samples were unrelated to memory.

They'll have to put it all back. Whatever it takes.

Harland tossed the photo back onto the desk and rubbed his eyes. The glossy slid a few inches, revealing another image just beneath. He brushed the first photo aside and picked up the second. A second still frame of camera footage, it showed the same chamber, but with greater clarity. The fog that obscured the previous photo had mostly faded from view, revealing more of the chamber.

Harland held it up to the light and licked his lips. "What fresh hell is this?" he muttered.

Chapter 4

Devil in the Details

Another red circle had been drawn around a figure that stood atop the platform in the distance, a tall humanoid with horns crowning its head like a demon straight out of hell. The black-and-white photo did not show it, but Harland imagined the thing's skin to be fire-red.

Skin colour aside, it looked different from the fire entities. Taller, more malevolent, and intelligent. Well muscled. Judging by the position of the energy ball behind it as it stood on the dais, it must be seven feet tall at least. Harland could not be sure, but he thought he saw flames coming from the horns on its head as it stared into the camera as if it knew the device was there.

It looked…biblical.

He wasn't especially religious; he hadn't gone to church regularly in years, but he had throughout his childhood, usually under duress (what kid wouldn't rather be playing with his friends?). In his view, religion wasn't about worshipping a creator; he doubted one existed. If it turned out to be true, that would be a bonus…but if one did, he felt certain of its indifference to humanity.

No, for Harland you went to church for the same reason you went to football games: community. Going increased your bond with your neighbours and family, your tribe. You needed to show those around you that you were on their side, that you shared and cared about what they did. To be a part of the group, you believed, or at least pretended to, no matter how much doing so defied probability.

Now, looking at this creature, he was wondering if maybe there was more to it than parables, morality, and historical distortions.

He picked up the phone and dialled. A voice answered on the second ring. He'd expected no less; Bodhi Group staff often worked odd hours, even more so this past week. Harland had not slept in days himself.

"Sean Peterson," said the voice on the other end.

"Hey, Sean. Dixon here."

"Back already?"

"Yeah," Harland said, "something came up. I'm calling about the chamber stills you sent over."

"Oh, good," Sean said. "I wasn't sure you'd get them tonight. I just dropped them off an hour ago. You were right. He was there."

"Nice job," Harland replied. He held the second photo up to the light. "What about this other one?"

"Ah, yes," Sean said, his voice rising. "We happened upon that while looking for Winterboy."

"The chamber is almost clear in the shot. Why didn't we see this in the video recording?"

"I know, right? The answer is a bit bizarre."

"And that is?"

"The figure appears in only four consecutive frames. Not quite at the subliminal level, but brief enough to miss when skimming the feed."

"How's that possible?"

Sean expelled a puff of air, audible over the phone line. "I wish I knew. My guess? Either it moved out of the camera's field of view faster than a speeding bullet or it simply vanished in an instant."

"Could the feed have been altered?"

"I don't see how," Sean replied. "The rest of the action is continuous and dynamic. If nothing had been moving in the room at the time, I'd say it having been altered is likely, but for the movement of the remaining fog and other entities to have been blended from frame to frame in the time since the recording was made is almost as unlikely as the other explanations."

"But it's possible?"

"Yeah, sure," Sean said. "But why bother?"

Harland sighed. "Beats me."

"Well," Sean said, "anything's possible…I guess. We'll give it another look, see if we can find any signs of tampering."

"All right," Harland replied. "Thanks. Let me know if you find anything else."

He returned the handset to its cradle and studied the photo again. Despite having suggested it, he somehow doubted Sean and his crew would find anything to indicate tampering.

He leaned back in his chair and rubbed his eyes. He had not slept more than eight hours in the days since Shivurr's escape. He'd been too busy interviewing Bodhi Institute denizens, trying to figure out what had happened.

He looked at his watch. The captives were not due to arrive for a while yet.

Just enough time for a quick power nap. He put his feet on his desk and closed his eyes. As a CIA field agent, he had quickly learned to sleep when opportunity allowed during crises. You never knew when you would next get a chance. It was even more important these days; all-nighters seemed to hit him harder lately. *The joys of aging,* he thought, as he drifted off to sleep.

He jumped in his chair as the phone rang sometime

later. His hand shot across the desk like a viper to snatch the receiver from the hook.

"Di…Dixon," he said before clearing his throat.

"They've arrived," Cynthia said. "Springer and Collins are putting them in a conference room, as you requested."

He stood. "Have they been any trouble?"

"Springer's got a shiner," Cynthia replied. "I guess the kids fought back when they grabbed them from Scott's house."

Harland raised his eyebrows, pursing his lips. "Hmm…we've got fighters on our hands. Good for them."

She chuckled. "I'm not sure Springer would agree with you."

"And the microphones?"

"Already in place."

"Good," Harland said. "Get them something to eat."

"Don't you want to talk to them?"

"Let them stew for a few hours; that'll give them time to think about what's coming, and hopefully say something that they shouldn't. I'll question them individually after they've had time to sweat a bit. Just be sure we're recording everything that they say, and have someone listen in real time and note anything that they say about Winterboy."

"Of course. Shall I call you in a few hours, then?"

"Sure," Harland replied. "If I don't answer, page me."

"Where will you be?"

"The gym."

Sometime later, Harland tossed a wet towel into a nearby hamper and began to dress. A few miles on the treadmill, followed by a cold shower, had beaten back his bone-weary fatigue, for now. He would have to sleep eventually, but it'd keep until after he got what he needed from the detainees. He knew from years of pushing himself that he had not yet reached his limits.

He shrugged into his suit jacket, custom-made to allow extra room under his left armpit for a shoulder holster. He patted the 9mm semi-auto cradled within, then checked his pockets for keys, employee badge, key card, and other incidentals. Checking his hair in a nearby mirror, he stroked his freshly shaven chin. Tired eyes looked back at him. He slapped his face, then strode for the door.

A few cups of coffee and he'd be good until morning. With that goal in mind, he made his way to the nearest break room, equipped with a small kitchenette, including a fridge for people's lunches, coffee makers, and a collection of vending machines. He stretched his calves and touched his toes, waiting for a fresh pot to brew, then grabbed a mug and poured. Disdaining sugar, he drank it black.

"Some fucking kid," said a voice from behind Harland as he drained his mug, wincing as the too-hot liquid slid down his throat.

Harland reached for the pot to refill it. "What's up, Springer?" he said without turning.

"Oh, hey," Springer said. "Didn't see you there, boss."

Harland put the pot back on the element and turned. Springer walked over, trailed by one of the computer systems guys, whose name he could not remember.

He thrust a chin at Springer's eye. "Telling war stories."

Springer shrugged as the tech made for the fridge. "He asked."

"Doesn't look too bad," Harland said. "Put some ice on it. It'll keep the swelling down."

"Hope they're worth the trouble," Springer replied, grabbing a mug from the counter. "Have you interrogated them yet?"

"Soon." Harland sipped his drink and swallowed. "Did they say anything?"

"Not to me." Springer filled his mug. "I haven't talked

to them since we tossed them in the back of the truck."

"They must have said *something* on the way."

"Maybe," Springer said. "I rode shotgun, though. Anything they said to the guys in the back should be in the report."

"Who's writing it up?"

"Kellerman."

Harland groaned inwardly. "Why him?" He had waded through Kellerman's rambling, incoherent reports before. Usually, he had to resort to debriefing the security agent in person to make sense of them.

Springer took a sip of his coffee. "You know how it is…you wait in the truck while the team goes in, you write the report."

"All right." Harland glanced at his watch. "If you think of anything else, let me know."

"Will do, sir."

Harland left the room, taking the still-steaming coffee mug with him.

Chapter 5

He'll Come

Harland rode the elevator up to subfloor two. Nodding to a janitor mopping the floor as he exited, he turned right, making his way toward Security Control Room One.

He lingered at the doorway, sipping his coffee. *You can learn a lot loitering near doorways now and then*, he thought, *including whether people are doing their jobs.*

"I'm just saying, monks aren't saints," said a voice that Harland recognized as belonging to Tom Lattimer, a thirty-something five-year member of the Bodhi Institute's security force.

"If you say so," replied a nasally voice.

Jason Mathis, Harland thought. Late twenties, he'd joined the team just six months earlier.

"You know some bald bastard came up with tonsures, right?" Harland imagined a barely suppressed smirk on Lattimer's face.

"How'd you figure?" Mathis said.

"Trust me," Lattimer began, "some punk kid snickered at his old abbot's sunburned pate. Next thing you know…he's rocking the *stupidest* fucking hairstyle in all of recorded history."

Mathis snickered. "I suppose that explains eunuchs."

"Not sure that's a monk thing," Lattimer said as Harland slipped inside, "but, uh…yeah, the same principle probably applies." The older guard continued to stare ahead, gaze alternating between the mainframe terminal that sat on the counter in front of him and the array of TV screens decorating the far wall, oblivious to his boss's arrival.

Harland held a finger to his lips as a third man, sitting across the room, looked up and saw him.

Mathis ran his fingers through his hair. "Better not hassle Dixon about his grey hair, then."

"Are you kidding?" Lattimer said. "I'd kill to have his hair, grey or…I don't know…purple."

"Better buy some hair dye, boys," Harland said.

Mathis jerked in his chair. "Holy!" he shouted, spinning toward the door.

Lattimer made a choking sound and spewed a fresh sip of coffee back into his mug, somehow managing not to spill any. "Trying to give me the big one, chief?" he said, wiping his chin.

"Grey hair is mandatory," Harland continued, "starting next week. Thanks for the idea."

Lattimer rubbed a hand across his bare scalp, leaving a damp smear from his still-wet palm, and chuckled. "Not sure there's enough left to bother."

"Might need to buy a wig," Harland said.

Mathis cackled. "You'd look hilarious."

Lattimer scowled and pointed a finger. "Just watch the friggin' monitors, smartass."

Both men returned their attention to the screens, occasionally tapping keyboards, sitting straighter than they had when he'd first walked in.

Harland approved.

They were good men, but getting fat from watching monitors and eating chips all day. Short and thick, Lattimer resembled a forty-year-old preschooler. Mathis, the younger of the two, already showed the start of a paunch as he slouched in his chair. Harland had more than twenty years on them but would run them both into the ground in a foot race. For that reason and more, they'd never be anything other than security officers.

It was no surprise, really. Not everyone had what it took to rise to the rank of Special Agent or even that of Field Agent. Bodhi Group Special Agents—the name, Harland presumed, borrowed from the FBI—served a similar function within the Group to their federal counterparts. Their main duties involved background checks, investigations, and counter-intelligence, but they also often served as bodyguards for high-ranking dignitaries or conducted special operations. But you didn't start out as an agent. Except for new hires with equivalent experience and rank in other agencies, you had to start at the bottom and rise to the elite ranks by putting in your time and distinguishing yourself.

Most future agents started as members of the Group's Security Protective Service, assisting with security and defense. Much of that service involved watching monitors, checking IDs, and guard and patrol duties. Exactly the sort of work that the two men were doing now.

Aside from the few management career paths available in the SPS, ambitious personnel sought to progress and distinguish themselves as Special Response Team members. An elite tactical branch of the SPS, the SRT provided rapid armed response in high-risk situations. In theory, the men could apply, but SRT units were dominated by younger men with an energy these two had likely never had.

That was fine. Everyone contributed in their own way. Nonetheless, he still demanded a high standard of his security officers. *They aren't mall cops; they're goddamn security specialists.*

Harland joined them in scrutinizing the monitors that covered the far side of the room, displaying interior and exterior scenes from around the Institute.

The main road in showed empty and dark.

"Anything worth reporting?"

Lattimer shook his head. "It's been quiet, boss. *Keine Probleme.*"

"What's that?" Harland asked. "German?"

"Yep," Lattimer replied. "New wife's from there."

Harland's nostrils flared, thinking of the alimony he'd paid over the years to his ex-wife, which she took far too happily for his liking. They had been childhood sweethearts and imagined their love eternal. *At least I did.* It had ended after he'd entered the CIA.

"We're going there to meet her parents next summer."

"If you're serious," Harland said, "you need to practise with someone fluent."

"Yeah," Lattimer agreed. "Emmett, the shrink, is helping me with that."

Mathis guffawed. "Nice cover," he said, swirling an index finger by his temple.

Lattimer scowled at Mathis. "Don't be an…*Arschloch.*"

"All right," Harland said, "all right. Settle it down." He smirked. "Lattimer's *mental* problems are his business."

Mathis cackled as Lattimer snorted and hung his head, shaking it almost imperceptibly. "You fucking guys…"

"You know we hassle you because we like you," Harland said, fake-punching Lattimer's shoulder. He emptied the last of his mug and placed it on a nearby table. "Who's listening to the group from Vegas?"

A hand shot up from across the room. The third man, Darryl Roberts, slipped aside one of the earpieces of his headphones, the headband of which lay hidden within his thick afro, as Harland approached. "That'd be me."

"Have they said anything interesting?"

Darryl smiled, giving Harland a sidelong look. "Like

Winterboy's current coordinates?"

"Now wouldn't that be nice." Harland lowered himself into a chair and slid closer. "Set me up so I can review what they've said so far. I want to hear everything."

"Roger that. It'll take a few minutes. I'll need to switch some tapes around."

"That's fine," Harland said. "I'll wait."

Several minutes later, Darryl handed him headphones and gestured at the equipment.

"I've set the tape to just before they first speak. They talk for a while, then it's silence after their food arrives."

Harland placed the headphones over his head and pressed the play button. He listened.

After a moment's silence, Harland winced as a rumbling belch sounded in his earpieces.

"That's disgusting," said the voice of a young girl.

"Every bodily function is disgusting," said an adolescent male voice, presumably the source of the belch.

"No, it isn't," insisted the girl.

"Shitting," the boy said.

"Well, obviously."

"Spitting?"

"No duh," the girl said.

"Farting." This came from someone else. Male, older.

"Uh, yeah," said the girl.

"Coughing?" said the boy.

"Well, not in my face!"

"Seriously?" said a second female voice. Still young, but somewhat older, more mature, a woman. "This is what you're talking about now?"

"Chewing with your mouth open," the boy continued.

"Well, we're not animals for God's sake," said the girl. "God, you're such a *boy* sometimes!"

"Sweating?" said the younger male again.

"Um, hello?" said the older female. "Am I talking to my-self?"

"It's just so smelly and moist." Harland imagined the younger girl's face scrunched in disgust.

"Jerking—"

"Ugh," the girl said. The sound of a slap followed. "Gross."

"Ouch!" The boy laughed. "That's my *sore* shoulder."

She giggled. "Serves you right."

"I think you're proving his point," said the other male.

"Hey, I got this defending you," the boy protested.

Ah, the kid that gave Springer his black eye. Harland smiled. *Smart, take your friends' minds off the situation with inane chatter.*

Harland hit a button, accelerating the playback.

As expected, their conversation transitioned to a discussion of their predicament and yielded little useful information aside from their first names. He presumed that the detainees' IDs would have been confiscated and the details included in Kellerman's report, but it would be useful knowledge if they hadn't had ID with them when they'd been taken.

He increased the playback to double speed, listening for anything of value. A long period of silence followed. His eyelids drooped, bounced like a garage door struggling to open, then snapped wide again. He stopped the tape, rewound it, then played it forward at normal speed so it didn't sound like a meeting of Alvin and the Chipmunks.

"Shivurr will save us," said the younger girl's voice.

Burp-boy replied, "I don't know. He risked his life to get away from here…"

"Doesn't matter. He'll come."

Well, there you go, Harland thought. *They know him.* Not only knew him, but well enough that the girl expected him to mount a *rescue*.

The conversation stopped. The conference room door swung open and thumped as someone entered.

"All right, kiddies," said a voice. "Got you some drinks and sandwiches."

Carlson, Harland thought, recognizing the voice of one of his men.

The captives made no reply.

The clink of bottles and thump of food trays being placed on the conference room table followed.

"Chatty bunch," Carlson said. "This silent treatment shit isn't going to cut it when Dixon gets around to talking with you. Do yourselves a favour and tell him whatever he wants to know."

Harland stopped the tape. Planting an elbow on the desk, he rested his chin between his thumb and forefinger. *Can it be true? Will Shivurr return to get these friends?*

He'd have to ask the head shrink, Feldman—the one they'd brought in to treat Shivurr—about it. *All that time the old man spent psychoanalyzing him has got to be worth something.* Harland sneered. He had little patience for psychobabble. *As if moaning on about your problems is going to do anything but make them worse.*

It was hard to believe Shivurr would risk returning when he'd done so much to escape, but Harland couldn't discount the possibility. If it was true, these four might be the break for which he'd been waiting.

It depended on Shivurr knowing that they had his young friends, of course. If not, there'd be no rescue attempt.

Does he know? He made a mental note to extract that particular nugget of information during their interrogations. *Even if Shivurr does know, he isn't stupid.* He wouldn't try a frontal assault. No, whatever he did, it would be stealthy, so they would need to be on high alert. And if no rescue attempt came, it seemed a good bet that these kids could at least steer him in Shivurr's direction. If he could get close enough, he'd tell Shivurr the news himself. *Use it to convince him to come back voluntarily.*

He turned to Roberts, who sat a few feet away, still listening to the live microphone. "I'm at the point where they're being fed."

"Uh-huh," Roberts said, tucking a headphone behind his ear.

"It's just silence after that?"

"Pretty much," Roberts said. "Whatever they say after is too far from the mikes or too faint for them to pick up. At least so far."

"You think they found them?"

"Dunno." Roberts's mouth gaped wide enough for Harland to see his uvula wiggling at the back of his throat. "Maybe…or they just suspect there's one. Then again, could be they're sleeping. It's pretty late."

Harland stifled his own yawn. "True."

He stared at the monitor showing the archival vault, which contained the most important and secret research and artifacts that the Bodhi Group possessed.

The place holding Shivurr's stolen essence.

Can its lure and these kids be enough to draw Shivurr back here? Harland doubted it, but then, he hadn't believed that the snowman would dare escape into the desert.

His gaze drifted absently across the bank of monitors. Movement on one caught his eye. A military truck, headlights on, rumbled down a ramp at the back of Institute to the loading bays.

He tapped Mathis, the guard to his right, with the back of his hand. "Is that truck bringing the dais from Alpha site?"

Mathis grunted. "Nope. *They* rolled in a while back. This

one's coming from Gamma."

"Carrying what? They can't be done there yet."

"Jimenez and crew," Mathis said. "The troops you requested showed up to take over, so they said they'd hitch a ride back."

"That's good," Harland said. "We need them here."

He had special agents spread across four states, searching for Shivurr, chasing down leads, coordinating with local law enforcement, and interviewing potential witnesses. Others like Jimenez's unit had been deployed to protect research sites from fire entity raids. Casualties suffered in those incursions had further thinned their ranks. The consequent double shifts and long hours had frayed the edges on the alertness of the Institute's remaining defenders. He'd had no choice but to submit a request for military reinforcement. With those soldiers now stepping in to protect and assist in dismantling research sites, Harland would soon have enough people on hand to properly protect the facility. He would have preferred not to involve outsiders, but with another two agents now in a Las Vegas hospital ICU, he was glad that he hadn't waited to do so.

Harland watched as Jimenez and several other security agents hopped off the back of the truck. An untidy mess at present, the loading dock swelled with crates of soda pop. Some held empties awaiting transport offsite, others full bottles awaiting transfer to cafeterias for consumption.

With Shivurr gone, the Bodhi Group's going to save a small fortune on pop, he mused. *Half those empties are probably his.*

Harland's eyebrows rose as Gary Ashdon leaped down from the idling truck. The new chemist turned to assist two other lab-coated men in disembarking. The trio grabbed metal cases from the back of the truck, then followed the rest of the passengers inside.

Harland pushed himself to his feet. "All right," he said

to the room, "keep me informed." He hadn't expected any of the researchers to return for several hours yet. He looked again at the monitor showing the archival vault. Whatever the reason for the academics' early return, a chemist was exactly what he needed right now. "If you hear or see anything significant, page me."

Roberts snugged his headphones back into place, giving Harland a wry grin. "Like Winterboy's—"

"Exact coordinates, yes," Harland said, "or something like that."

"Going to start the interviews?" Lattimer asked without turning.

"Not yet," Harland murmured. "I've got something to take care of first."

"Later, boss," Mathis said as he left.

Chapter 6

Elemental Alchemy

Harland found Ashdon on subfloor fifteen, next to one of the chambers housing the fire entities. He stared through the viewing port as if hypnotized, with his mouth ajar.

"Pretty freaky, eh?" Harland said.

Ashdon whirled. "Shit."

"Easy," Harland said, chuckling. "It's just me."

Ashdon flinched as a fireball struck the reinforced window next to him with a thump. "Sorry," he said, glancing back at the holding cell. "I didn't hear you coming."

"I imagine you were distracted," Harland said as one of the entities glided over to the window to regard them in turn. "They're a bit mesmerizing…like staring down the throat of a volcano. Another Red Menace this country now has to face."

"As if the Soviets weren't enough," Ashdon said with a wry smile. He pressed a palm against the glass as another sphere flared against the window. "I'm glad I'm not on the other side of this wall."

"You wouldn't last a minute," Harland said. "At least not without a fire suit."

Ashdon patted the pockets of his lab coat. "I seem to have left mine behind in the move."

"No worries," Harland said. "We've got you covered. There's a bunch in storage on this level." He pointed a thumb over his shoulder in the direction from which he'd come. "All levels with research labs have them."

"I guess you'd need them," Ashdon replied. "You must deal with this sort of thing a lot."

"Yep," Harland agreed. "We're well equipped for fighting fires. Not because of these guys, though."

"I suspected not," Ashdon said. "I imagine it'd take the nearest fire department far too long to get here."

"Well, that *and* these levels are top secret. We can't have firemen running through the halls. Nope. If fire breaks out here, it's up to us to deal with it. With some of the experiments being conducted here, fire's a common occurrence." He rested a palm against the glass. "That's why we've got firefighting equipment on most levels, extinguishers placed throughout, and a state-of-the-art fire suppression system."

"I don't doubt it," Ashdon said. "These organisms just upped your fire risk level into the red zone."

"*That* they have…but you can rest easy, Ashdon, we're fully fireproofed."

Ashdon gazed at Harland over the top of his eyeglasses. "Like the *Titanic* was iceberg-proof?"

Harland chuckled. "Unlike the *Titanic*, this isn't the Institute's maiden voyage. Crises are normal around here."

Ashdon leaned a shoulder against the wall opposite the entities' enclosure. "You might want to add mention of that to the internal job postings."

Harland scoffed. "I'll pass that along to HR." He turned to study the smaller man. "You *must* have some stories to tell from your last job, though. Life in the Group is seldom boring."

"I suppose I've got a few."

"Drop by my office sometime and we can trade war stories," Harland said. He glanced over his shoulder, then back to Ashdon, and cupped a hand to the side of his mouth. "I keep a bottle of scotch locked in my desk," he said in a hushed voice.

"I appreciate the welcome," Ashdon said. "I'm not much of a drinker, though."

Harland waved a hand dismissively. "Your loss." His face grew serious. "So, what brings you down?"

Ashdon flicked the access card hanging from a badge holder at his waist. "I *had* to take a look after you told me I'd been given access."

Harland lifted his eyebrows. "Is that why you came back from the site so soon?"

Ashdon's face reddened. "No, not really." He shrugged. "We did what we could under the conditions, but even with flashlights and lanterns, it was difficult to see, so we're waiting for morning to continue."

"Told you," Harland said with a smirk.

"That you did," Ashdon said, nodding. "Though we did find the residue of several fire elementals even so."

"Elementals," Harland said, uttering the word as if he'd just discovered ten down on the Sunday crossword puzzle. "I *like* that. We've just been calling them entities, which is a bit generic and vague. Fire *elementals*. What made you call them that?"

"Oh, well…I…uh," Ashdon said. "I don't really know. It just seemed to fit." He cleared his throat. "In any case, with the military transport returning to the Institute, I saw an opportunity to bring the samples back for safekeeping."

"I'm glad that you did," Harland said. "I need your help with something, if you're willing."

Ashdon licked his lips. "What do you need?"

"Don't look so nervous. It should be child's play for a chemist like yourself."

"Well, my PhD is in biochemistry, but I *do* have an

undergraduate degree in chemistry."

"What's the difference?"

"Biochemists study chemical processes as they relate to living organisms. Chemistry is more…general."

"Ah, right." Harland nodded. "You're here to study Winterboy's biochemistry, then?"

"I hope so. If he can be recovered. I've studied some of the extracts taken from him in the past. It's been a rare privilege. The presence of stable, energetic quasicrystals in his makeup is particularly—"

"Then you know what the samples look like, right? Their consistency, colour, and iridescence."

"Of course."

Harland raised the bottle that he'd grabbed from one of the Institute's many labs while searching for Ashdon. He'd also stopped by his office to pick up something else required for his plan. "Do you think you can mix me up something that looks similar to a Winterboy sample in this?"

Ashdon grasped the bottle and held it up to the light. "Hmm…it depends on what we've got on hand for the mix, but I can probably create something that should be reasonably close. I might need to visit the cafeteria for a few ingredients."

"When can you have it ready?"

Ashdon checked his watch. "It shouldn't take long. Maybe a half hour. An hour at most."

"Perfect," Harland said.

"What, may I ask, is this for? If Dr. Huggins should ask what I've been up to…I'd like to be able to tell her."

"It's a long shot," Harland began, "but it's something to help us find Winterboy. If it works, you'll be quite the hero, Ashdon."

"I'll get right on it, then."

"Good man," Harland said. "Lead the way."

"You're coming with me?"

"Yup," Harland replied. "This is top priority."

Forty minutes later, Ashdon handed Harland the test tube, filled three-quarters of the way to its top. Bowls, bottles, and packaging lay strewn across the chemistry lab countertop, one of several arranged in neat rows across the classroom-sized room. Harland studied the liquid inside, comparing it with his memories of the real samples taken from Shivurr over the past several years.

"It's not a perfect match," Ashdon said, "but should be good enough."

"Either way," Harland said, "it'll have to do…this isn't acidic or poisonous, is it?"

Ashdon shook his head. "The taste will probably leave something to be desired, but, no, nothing toxic or caustic."

Harland pulled a tracking device—collected from a drawer in his office—from the breast pocket of his jacket. Holding it over the bottle like a magician performing a trick, he lowered it in, careful to avoid spillage. A few inches long and about a half inch wide, the waterproof tracker sank without touching the sides. Displaced liquid threatened to spill over the bottle's rim.

He eyeballed the stopper, holding it next to the bottle, then dumped some of the concoction into a nearby sink, sealed the bottle, and rinsed the exterior.

"What did you put inside?" Ashdon asked, wiping down the counter and returning containers to shelves and cabinets.

"A surprise," Harland said, "for our escaped snowman, if he should be crazy enough to return here."

Ashdon paused and stared. "You think he'll return on his own? Why would he do that?"

Harland gazed toward the ceiling. "Some friends of his

are upstairs in one of the conference rooms. They seem to think he'll come for them."

"Do you think he'll take that risk?"

"Probably not. Not *just* for them, no, but he might to get what we took from him."

"The material samples that were extracted from him?"

"Exactly."

"But I'd understood Winterboy no longer recalls many of the things done to him." Ashdon knuckled his eyes. "How would he know that they even exist?"

Harland shrugged. "He had *help* getting away from here. *Inside* help. At this point…there's no telling what he knows or what the person or persons helping him may have told him." *And*, Harland thought, *he returned to Alpha site. He knew it existed and how to find it, so either he remembers more than we thought, or* someone's *filled in the gaps for him.*

"Aren't the samples stored in a secure location?" Ashdon asked, sliding a cabinet door shut before flopping back onto his stool. He removed his spectacles and laid them on the counter before him. Putting his elbows onto the counter, he folded his arms into makeshift pillows and rested his head on his forearms.

"Of course," Harland said. "In the archival vault, behind a thick steel door." Ashdon murmured something Harland couldn't quite hear. "What's that?"

"I don't see how he could possibly get in," Ashdon said into his arms in a louder voice.

"Agreed," Harland said. "More likely it'll be whoever helped him to flee. Either way, I want to cover my bases."

"Should you be telling me this, then? Aren't you worried I'm the traitor? I mean, I'm not, but—"

"You're one of the few people that I can be sure *isn't* the traitor. You just got here."

Ashdon lifted his head to regard Harland. "Ah, so that's

why you didn't ask one of the other chemists on staff."

"Pretty much." Harland flashed a smile. "Plus, it's late. No sense waking people unnecessarily. I'm nice that way."

"Well," Ashdon said, "I'm glad that I could help. I'd hate for those samples to be lost. They're my whole reason for being here."

"Don't worry, Ashdon. Once I slip this in with the others, the best thing that could happen is someone taking them. Because then I'll have them right where I want them."

"Do you want more—in case they don't grab that one? There's plenty of solution left over."

"Nah," Harland said. "Too many fake ones may tip them off."

"What about putting trackers in the real ones?"

Harland snorted. "No chance. I don't want to contaminate them." He pointed at the sink. "Besides, I'd have to dump some solution to make them fit."

"Right," Ashdon replied, looking thoughtful. "Good point. Too bad…"

"Don't worry. If someone comes for them, they're not going to leave any containers behind. Of course, we'll do everything we can to catch them before they make it that far. This is just a fail-safe." Harland's pager beeped. He thumbed the buttons and squinted at the display. "All right, I've got to go."

"I can take those to the vault for you, if you've got to deal with something."

"Thanks," Harland said, pushing himself to his feet, "but don't sweat it. You don't have access. Few do. Get some rest. You look exhausted."

"Tell me about it," Ashdon said, glancing at the clock on the wall. He slid from the stool. "I'm returning to Gamma site in the morning, so I probably *should* retire." He looked around. "I just have a bit more cleaning up to do."

"I'll leave you to it," Harland said. "Thanks for your help."

"Good luck," Ashdon said, watching as Harland left the room.

Chapter 7

Intruder Alert

He made his way down the corridor, heading for the vault. He'd answer the page as soon as the potion that he and Ashdon had concocted lay safely ensconced with the others. If the traitor or traitors hadn't helped Shivurr purely out of sympathy to his situation, then they were most likely enemy spies, and there was no telling when they might act.

He drew up short as he entered the hall that lay near the centre of the building: a large open area that spanned three floors, known to the Institute denizens as the Agora. Sofas, benches and low tables had been shoved to the edges, creating a clearing near the middle. The dais that had been discovered near Alpha site stood within a translucent cage of glasslike material. Ductwork and fans attached to the cage blew cold air into the box and warmer air out, refrigerating the interior. Harland didn't know the precise reasons for it but understood that temperature played a part in the scientific research being conducted on the daises, and within the Alpha site chamber itself.

He drifted closer to the glass box and studied the words inscribed on the stony surface of the platform. His rusty Latin deciphered only some of the words: *ET*, *AD*, *TERRA*, *VENITE*—AND, TO, EARTH, COME. Others looked Latin as well but were otherwise undecipherable. Among the text, carvings of alien symbols and glyphs, unlike anything he'd ever seen, glowed an eerie blue, as if painted with radium like the dials on old watches.

While the Alpha site chamber's art and architecture included Ancient Greek *and* Roman influences, Latin remained the only identifiable language carved into the stone within, implying that the chamber had been constructed during the heyday of the more recent of the two great civilizations. Yet the writings described items and conveyed concepts more reminiscent of Ancient Greece.

He wondered what the linguists made of it all: the unknown characters in particular. He made a mental note to look into it. It wasn't exactly relevant to his position, but he didn't like not knowing. Being able to get answers and observe fascinating phenomena was a perk of the job, allowing and compelling him to interact with Shivurr more than he might have otherwise.

In the early days, to everyone's delight, they had discovered Shivurr spoke *Latin*, in addition to his native tongue. The latter, incredibly, something *no one* had heard before.

Given his proficiency with Latin, Harland bet that Shivurr could have translated the words on the dais himself…if someone had thought to ask him before they'd started extracting his memories. *Once that nasty shit started, reminding the poor bastard of his origins would have been counterproductive…besides, how useful could a translation be?* It wasn't likely to be instructions on how to cure cancer or the answer to life, the universe, and everything, like in that radio play his brother's kid had played for everyone last Thanksgiving.

He tried to recall the name.

Hitcher's something, he thought. *Whatever it was, Jacob sure got a kick out of it.*

He was a good kid, even if not much of an athlete. It was a shame that his parents were spoiling him, though.

Filling his head with socialist garbage. Unlike Harland, the boy would never know what it was like to grow up with nothing. Jacob had gotten more gifts last Christmas than Harland had in a dozen Christmases of his own youth.

As a child of the Great Depression, Harland had entered adolescence around the time that the United States had entered World War Two. He *knew* poverty. He *knew* that the world owed you nothing and cared about you even less than that. He knew how bad things could get and that you had to work hard and be prepared to *fight* to survive and keep what was yours.

Socialism sounded good in theory, but ultimately Harland knew that it suited only the lazy. Those who couldn't be happy, regardless of their economic status, if anyone had more than them, no matter if others worked harder and saved more for what they had…and they certainly weren't prepared to work harder themselves. And it wasn't about rich or poor. He knew lazy and driven people across the economic scale. He'd grown up poor himself but still believed in the American dream.

Harland's younger brother's ideals snarled his stomach into knots when he let himself think about them. They'd had pretty much the same upbringing, but somehow Michael had fallen victim to the socialist con. Maybe he felt he had to rebel against their father (who despised communism) or distinguish himself from Harland (who agreed with their father).

Who knows, he thought, scowling. *More likely, the hippies are responsible.*

His younger brother had grown up with the kumbaya bullshit, and living with the threat of the draft *must* have been rough. Even now in 1983, with the Vietnam War well over, the ideas that had begun with the longhairs still lingered across the country. Not just lingered, but seemed to gather strength.

He sympathized with the general idea. *No one sane* wants *to go to war.*

When he thought about the things he'd seen *over there*, he felt lucky that Michael had managed to avoid that. Let his little brother live his life. Harland had already contributed enough to the causes of this country for both of them, even if his brother lacked the sense and grace to appreciate it.

He checked his watch. *Time to get moving.* He bumped a fist against the glass, then turned away, breaking into a trot after a few steps. He made his way through the maze of corridors, slowing to a brisk walk when passing the few other people still moving about on the level. Arriving at the vault entrance, he used his access card to get past the outer set of bars. Beyond them, the massive vault door, over a foot thick, hung wide, and he entered the vault proper—a large cave carved out of the earth itself—unhindered.

It must have taken years to carve out such a large space, he thought, as he often did upon entering. *You could probably fill it with the dollar bills it cost to make it as well.* He smiled. *Then again, the same can be said for the entire facility—more so, in fact.*

The walls were left natural, but they'd surfaced the floor using the same grey-and-black tile paving the hallways of much of the rest of the Institute, laid out like an endless chessboard; *some sort of vinyl or plastic*, he guessed. Polished to a shine.

Most weeks he'd have been alarmed to find the portal open at this hour, but protocol allowed for the door to be left ajar during periods of high traffic. You couldn't get to the floor without access, and if you somehow made it that far, you'd be stopped at the outer bars. The vault door served mainly as a redundant protection, part of a defense in depth strategy, so relaxing protocol during extreme circumstances was only a small risk. *Besides, the vault door seals automatically in an emergency.*

With the recent attacks on Alpha and other sites, the archival vault played host to a parade of personnel as teams worked to move artifacts, data, and equipment to the Institute for safekeeping. Those items didn't stay in place long. They were soon checked out by scientists working long hours to analyze remnants of the Group's fiery new enemy.

Harland strolled down the row where Shivurr's samples lay, studying the contents through the glass fronts of the coolers until he found the right section. Cracking the door, he reached inside. Tendrils of fog drifted about him as the cold air within mixed with the warmer air of the cavern.

He pulled a tray of test tubes closer.

The unnatural glow of the substances that they contained confirmed that they were Shivurr's. He held the potion that Ashdon had prepared next to one.

Good enough, he thought.

It didn't look quite right but should pass casual inspection. The real ones varied in appearance anyway, so if his Trojan horse looked off, anyone grabbing them should chalk it up to natural variance.

He pulled out a pen and copied the text of a real potion—along with a made-up sample number—onto the label he'd affixed to the side of the fake one, then nestled the bottle in among the others, closed the door, and smiled.

"Time to get back," he said aloud as he turned to leave.

A clack echoed in the cave as if the hard sole of a dress shoe had tapped the floor, snapping Harland's head to the right.

"Hello?" Harland said. "Is someone there?"

No one answered.

He held still, trying to discern anything unusual over the hum of the ventilation system.

Hearing nothing more, he moved down the aisle in the direction of the sound.

Another footfall rapped against the floor.

Harland tiptoed at a jog toward the end of the aisle, wincing at each tap made by his shoes, and slipped his hand beneath his jacket. With practised ease, he used his thumb to pop the button of the strap securing his pistol. His fingers curled around the textured grip, squeezing the material like five mini pythons, and he tugged it free.

As it cleared the holster, pounding footsteps sounded from an adjacent aisle, moving in the direction of the exit. Abandoning stealth, he shot forward. He rounded the corner two aisles over, catching only the flash of a white lab coat as the runner cut to the left, breaking his line of sight.

"Hey," he shouted, skidding into a freezer door as he changed direction. "Stop right there."

Running footfalls were the only answer.

Harland picked up the pace. "Get your ass back here. You're just making this worse on yourself."

Turning as he reached the end of the aisle, he skated to the right, windmilling his arms. Bumping into a cabinet, he shoved against it, sending himself along a new vector of travel. He caught sight of the fugitive soon after, moving fast toward the vault door. Just a glimpse of white lab coat and black pants registered on his retinas before the intruder—as Harland now thought of him—vanished through the open portal.

"Goddamn it!"

Beads of sweat ran down his cheeks as he sprinted to catch up.

"You're starting to *piss*…me…OFF!"

The outer bars clanged as he neared the vault door.

Harland accelerated.

The angle of his approach would not afford him a view

of the outer bars or his quarry until he reached the opening itself. If he could identify the guy, the chase would be over. He'd have his men take him into custody, and Harland would interrogate him at his leisure.

He passed through the portal into the entrance hall seconds later.

It lay deserted.

He kept moving, determined to catch his prey in the halls. He raced down straightaways but approached corners with caution, gun raised in case of ambush. When he pulled to a stop at the nearest set of elevators without further sight nor sound of his target, his guts started to twist.

The lights were out above the elevator doors, so he checked the stairs. Craning his neck, he listened for footsteps, holding his breath even as his lungs screamed for more air, but he heard nothing.

After ten seconds, he moved back into the hallway. Bent over, hands on his knees and head lowered, he glanced down the corridor in both directions. He held his breath again, listening for the sound of movement, but heard only the blood rushing in his ears.

"Nuts," he said, slipping his pistol back into its holster. "When I find you, you're paying for my dry cleaning." His armpits felt damp and a trickle of sweat ran down his spine. "Goddamn it. I already went to the gym today."

He took off his jacket, draped it over his arm, and pulled a handkerchief from his breast pocket. He wiped the sweat from his brow, then slurped water from the drinking fountain that lay opposite the elevators.

Loosening his tie, he flopped onto a nearby bench. "You can run…I'll give you that."

His belt vibrated.

Laying his jacket to the side, he snatched his pager from its holder.

A number he knew well scrolled across the display. *The security control room.*

He smiled, thinking of the cameras and men that monitored the entrance to the vault 24-7. In the heat of the moment, he'd forgotten them.

"Oh, yes," he said. "You can run…but you can't hide."

He stabbed the elevator call button and boarded a minute later. He'd answer the page in person.

Whoever was playing cat-and-mouse games with him was about to lose.

Chapter 8

Technical Issues

Harland stopped short as he burst from the elevator onto the security control room's floor, grabbing Lattimer's shoulders to avoid bowling him over as the shorter man took a step back.

"Jesus," Lattimer said, wide-eyed.

"There you are," Harland said, brushing by the man. "Was that you that paged me?"

"Uh-huh," Lattimer replied. "I was coming to find you. The archival vault camera—"

"You saw, then?" Harland twisted his neck to regard Lattimer but kept walking. "The guy running from me?"

Lattimer rubbed his neck, lowering his eyes. "Well, not exactly, no."

"Don't sweat it," Harland said as Lattimer rushed to keep up. "We'll check the recording."

"That's why I came to find you," Lattimer said, already huffing for air.

"Good," Harland said. "I like the initiative. Whoever this guy is, he's fast…but not fast enough to avoid video cameras."

Lattimer cleared his throat. "That's what I wanted to tell you."

Harland thrust open the security control room door. "Mathis, I need to see the video recordings for the archival vault for the past thirty minutes, ASAP."

"That's what I wanted to tell you," Lattimer repeated from behind him. He gestured at the wall of monitors. Two of them showed black-and-white snow. "Some cameras stopped transmitting about twenty minutes ago."

"They cut out one or two at a time," Mathis said, throwing out his hands as if testing for rain, "then came back on after a few seconds."

"We didn't notice at first," Lattimer added.

"Why the hell not?"

"Too many cameras," Mathis said. "Not enough monitors; some displays alternate between video feeds for a few seconds at a time in sequence."

"Tell me something I don't know," Harland said. He stabbed a finger at one of the screens. "If they came back on, why are those still showing snow?"

"That's why we paged you," Lattimer said. "Some of the feeds went out and stayed that way. We noticed it with the vault camera feed first."

"It's got a dedicated display," Mathis explained, aiming a hand at one of the monitors. "It's considered too important to cycle."

"We gave it a few minutes," Lattimer said, "hoping it would come back online."

"When it didn't," Mathis said, "we paged you."

Harland's jaw clenched. "You're telling me we've got *nothing?*"

Lattimer hung his head. "Afraid so."

Harland sucked in a deep breath and held it for several heartbeats before letting it out slowly.

Lattimer's eyes flicked to his partner, then back to Harland. "You okay, boss?"

"Yeah…copacetic," Harland replied. His scowl morphed into a rueful grin. "I guess I picked a bad week to quit smoking."

Lattimer chuckled. "Looks like the *wrong* week all right."

Mathis's bushy eyebrows climbed his forehead. "*You* smoke?"

"Don't watch a lot of movies, Mathis?"

"*Airplane*," Lattimer said. Mathis stared blankly. "Are you shitting me? You haven't seen it?"

"Never mind," Harland said. "Have you sent someone to take a look?"

"We weren't sure who to call," Lattimer said. "Half the team's out looking for Winterboy. Most of the rest are asleep. We knew *you* were awake—waiting to talk to those kids—so figured we should talk to you first."

Mathis pointed a thumb over his shoulder. "We'd have sent Darryl to take a look, but he's busy…listening to those kids."

Roberts looked up at the mention of his name, raising his eyebrows in silent inquiry. Harland held up a hand and shook his head. Shrugging, the kid adjusted his headphones and returned to his surveillance.

"Could it be a glitch in the CCTV system?" Harland asked.

"Maybe," Lattimer said. "We've had cameras go down before. Usually it's a loose wire or signal interference coming from a nearby lab, but this many in succession, distributed across the facility…it's definitely unusual. What do you think, Jason?"

"I don't know," Mathis said, wobbling his head side to side. "Electromagnetic interference does degrade image quality, but this level of degradation would require a *major* EMI source."

Harland narrowed his eyes. "Like a deliberate signal jammer?"

"Could be," Lattimer agreed. "Maybe something that could be aimed…like a weapon."

"Yeah," Mathis interjected, "or someone's walking through the halls with one hell of a magnet in their pocket."

"All right," Harland began, "something's definitely hinky." He'd almost convinced himself that the guy in the lab coat had run from him for a laugh—the mystery man had gained access to the Institute's most secure area, so an authorized employee seemed likely—but camera trouble at the same time couldn't be a coincidence. Especially when it had all the earmarks of deliberate, albeit temporary, sabotage. It definitely rose beyond freaking out the director of security for laughs.

Harland grimaced. *It's got to be whoever helped Shivurr escape. They're up to something.* "Make me a list of the cameras that went out in chronological order."

A minute later, Mathis handed him a piece of paper. He studied the monitors, eyes flicking between each camera in sequence. They traced a vague path, starting near the fire entity enclosure, passing through the Agora, continuing past a bank of elevators, and ending at the archival vault.

The path I took to get there.

He hadn't checked his watch at the time but thought it likely they'd gone out around the time he'd made his way to the vault.

"Did you see me on the camera before this happened?"

"Don't think so," Lattimer said. He looked at Mathis. "Jason?"

Mathis ran his tongue beneath his upper lip and looked to the side. "Last I remember…you were staring at that thing in the Agora."

"Then they cut out before I left there."

"Maybe," Lattimer said. "We should be able to confirm that by reviewing the recordings, but it'll take a while." He extended a hand toward the screens. "But we can't watch the cameras at the same time."

"It can wait," Harland said. "Stay on—"

"Holy shit," Mathis said, pointing. "Another one just winked out."

"Where?" Harland said. His head snapped from image to image like a bird of prey looking for its next meal.

"The Agora," Mathis replied.

"I've had enough of this shit," Harland mumbled. He tapped a monitor on the far left. "That's Jimenez and his squad in the cafeteria. Get in touch with him. Tell him to bring his team to meet me at the Agora, ASAP."

"Roger, boss," Lattimer said, taking a seat and punching buttons on the telephone next to him.

"And tell them to come armed," Harland added.

Mathis leaned forward in his chair. "Do you want one of us to come with you?"

Harland waved him down, glancing at the wall of monitors, displaying dozens of video camera feeds. "No, stay here. Monitoring this many cameras is a two-person job. If you see any other cameras go out, page me. Otherwise, just keep watch for anything suspicious."

As the elevator descended to sublevel fifteen, Harland drew his weapon and held it at his side. Exiting, he crept along the hall toward the Agora, walking on the balls of his feet to keep the soles of his shoes from clicking on the hard floor. His footfalls still sounded, but he hoped that the refrigeration system running in the Agora would drown out his approach in a wash of white noise.

A blaze of light, accompanied by an electric crackle, flared from ahead of him. Harland ducked his head and scrunched his eyes. Stopping in his tracks, he thrust a hand against the wall for support.

The light strobed, changing from pure white to blue, then to green. Shouts rang out from somewhere ahead, just audible over the crackle of energy.

He cracked his right eye a sliver as the noise and light diminished before it faded away entirely. Pounding footsteps emerged from the new silence, growing louder by the second.

Blinking away the light's afterimage, Harland readied his weapon as a man and woman appeared. Scientists, by their dress. The man blond-haired, tall and lanky, mid-forties. *Gilbert something.* The woman heavyset, with curly brown hair, spun into a beehive atop her head. Probably a few years older than Harland. *Martha? No, Marilyn.*

They stumbled toward him, faces drawn, each trailing a hand along the wall as they scurried closer, lab coats fluttering.

"What's going on?" Harland grabbed the man's arm. "What the hell was that?"

Gilbert rubbed his eyes. "I don't know…the dais."

"It lit up like the sun," Marilyn said. "My eyes…I'm still having trouble seeing. Is that you, Harland?"

"Someone's in there," Gilbert said. He stole a glance over his shoulder. "In the refrigerated enclosure. I saw him in there, just before it…began to strobe."

"All right," Harland said. "Wait here." He pointed a finger at a nearby bench. "Take a seat before you fall down. Security is on the way."

"What are you going to do?" Gilbert said, flopping onto the bench and reaching out a hand to guide his companion onto the seat next to him.

Harland brandished his weapon. "My job."

Checking his weapon, he crept ahead, squinting his eyes in case the light show returned.

Within a hundred feet, the corridor spilled out into the Agora. Bulbs overhead flickered and faded, their failing glow no match for the waves of multicoloured light radiating from the dais dangling within the refrigerated chamber at the room's centre.

Harland scanned the area for threats. Finding none, he pattered across to the icebox and looked inside, blocking the glare of the dais with a hand.

"What the…," he whispered, pressing a palm to the glass and squatting. Slumped and lifeless on the floor inside sprawled an unmoving form—face down, wearing the de facto uniform of an Institute researcher: a knee-length white lab coat.

A wall of cold air raised goosebumps on Harland's flesh as he entered and rushed to the fallen man's side. Looking about the chamber and the larger room beyond, he grabbed the figure's wrist and checked for a pulse. Finding none, he turned the body over.

Gary Ashdon's unseeing eyes stared back at him.

Chapter 9

Power Trouble

Harland winced as blinding light flared from behind him, accompanied by the same electrical crackling sound that he'd heard in the hallway before encountering Gilbert and Marilyn.

Dimly, he recalled the flashlight he'd take camping as a kid. He'd cover the light with his hand and marvel at how the beam shone through, an orangey-red. Just as the skin and bone of his hand had failed to block the radiance of that hand torch, his eyelids were no match for the strobing kaleidoscope of illumination that emanated from the dais at his back.

Dropping his weapon, he pressed his palms to his eyes, scrunching his eyelids so hard that he imagined his brows touched his cheeks.

The electrical crackling grew, pounding in his ears. He ducked his head toward his torso, trying in vain to block out the sound with his shoulders. He staggered to his feet, determined to stumble his way out, when the bedlam mercifully receded. With his ears still ringing, he lowered his hands.

By the time spots no longer clouded his vision, the dais had returned to normal. He turned to leave and jumped, flailing his arms to his front at an unexpected tug on his pant leg.

"Dixon," said a voice.

Harland whirled to see Gary Ashdon push himself to an elbow and extend a hand.

"Holy mother!" Harland grabbed the scientist's cold hand and pulled him to his feet. "You…you…you had no pulse."

"I beg your pardon?" Ashdon dusted off his hands.

"You were lying here. I thought you were dead."

The scientist smoothed his lab coat, regarding Harland over the top of his eyeglasses. "That's demonstrably not the case."

Harland snorted. "Yeah, I guess so." He extended a hand. "Glad you're still with us."

Ashdon clasped the offered hand. "Me too." Pulling away, he glanced down and pointed at his feet, where Harland's weapon still lay. "Is that yours?"

"Oh, crap." Harland crouched, scooping his pistol from the floor, feeling a rush of blood to his cheeks. "Thanks. Must have dropped it when that light went off." He jammed it back into its holster. "What the hell happened here?"

"I'm not sure," Ashdon said, clutching the back of his neck and looking around. "I heard what sounded like a *massive* electrical short in this vicinity. I came to investigate and saw a sphere of white light hovering at the dais's side." He thrust a hand at the centre of the artifact. "Flashes of light…like electrical discharges, I thought, came from the sphere, striking the runes, making them glow brighter—"

Harland scowled. "And you thought it was a good idea to enter?" He smacked a hand to his forehead. "Didn't it occur to you that they put this thing in a box to protect people from whatever this thing does? For a smart guy, that's pretty fucking dumb."

Ashdon's face reddened. "Perhaps so." He glanced at the dais. "I suppose scientific curiosity overcame prudence.

Though, in my defense, the electrical phenomena, according to the research I've read, have been deemed to present no risk. Despite appearances, they're not electricity as we know it."

Harland scoffed. "Sure, they put it in a box because it's harmless."

Ashdon turned his palms to the ceiling. "It's my understanding that this container exists only to keep the dais from disappearing."

"Still…it's a crazy risk," Harland said. "Look, I don't mean to give you a hard time—you're new—but keeping you safe is my job. You boneheads don't make it easy. Have you *met* Wallace?"

"Well, no, not yet."

Harland hushed his voice. "The guy's a *professional* pain in the ass…and he loves his job."

Ashdon shivered and rubbed his arms. "Do you mind if we—"

"Yeah." Harland made a shooing gesture toward the exit. "Let's move before this thing acts up again." He closed the door to the booth and turned back to Ashdon. "If those electrical discharges don't present a risk, why were you lying on the floor, practically dead?"

"All I can recall is the light and sound grew painful in intensity. When the lights began strobing through the colour spectrum, I suppose I passed out."

"Passed out?"

"I have a condition," Ashdon replied. "Photosensitive—"

"Epilepsy," Harland said, thrusting a finger like a kid playing cops and robbers. "I remember now."

"You…*know*? Is that in my file? That's *supposed* to be confidential."

"Not from me," Harland said. "Anything that affects or

may affect the security of the Institute or its personnel—"

"How does that affect anything?"

"I don't know. Maybe some *fool* with a vulnerability to flashing lights decides to step into a box with a strobing light source and hits his head or something. It could happen." He snapped his fingers. "Oh, wait, it *did*..." He trailed off at the sound of pounding footsteps.

Moments later, Jimenez and three other security agents entered the room. Their weapons were raised as they scanned the room for threats. Spotting Harland and Ashdon, Jimenez lowered his weapon and approached. The men with him fanned out, adopting a standard defensive formation around the group in response to their leader's hand signals.

"What took you so long, Jimenez?" Harland barked. "Did you finish your coffee and donut first?"

"Sorry, *jefe*," Jimenez replied. "The fucking elevator stopped. Power failure, I guess."

Harland gaped. "Power failure?"

The Institute's electrical systems were robust and partitioned to protect against facility-wide blackouts. Wallace had ordered it after experiments had knocked out power to the entire facility one time too many. Nowadays, power failures were limited to a subset of floors and equipment, if they occurred at all. While not an electrical engineer, Harland felt sure that the elevators Jimenez and crew would have taken drew power from a different source than the Agora. If *they* had stopped, the loss of power extended further than he had thought.

"Anything else affected?"

Jimenez tossed his shoulders. "Not sure." He glanced at the other men. "We came straight here as soon as it started moving again. We didn't see anything on the way. But, like I said, the power was back on by then."

"It went out here too," Harland said. "Seemed more like a brownout than a full outage; like something was sucking it all up." He pointed a thumb over his shoulder in the direction of the dais. "I'm fairly sure that thing is the cause. Beats me how, though."

"Is that why you wanted us to come?" Jimenez asked.

"No…not exactly." Harland filled them in on recent events, including the sound and light show and finding Ashdon passed out in the chamber.

"Damn," Jimenez said. He looked at the dais sidelong. "You got some *cojones*, new guy." He crossed himself. "Bad shit happens near these things."

"Well," Ashdon replied, "I can certainly attest to that."

"Some say they're portals to hell," Jimenez continued, wide-eyed.

"Because of the incursions?" Ashdon asked.

"Sure," Jimenez agreed. "They're like something out of Dante's freaking *Inferno*, right?"

Ashdon looked thoughtful. "Except that involved a descent into hell," he said, "if I remember correctly. This is the other way around." He coughed. "As if hell is coming to earth."

"Jesus," Harland said, rolling his eyes. "Someone's seen *The Exorcist* a few times too many."

"It's *heh-soos*, Dixon," Jimenez said, flashing bright white teeth in a broad smile. "Good movie, though."

"Not *you*," Harland replied. "Different guy."

"Hey," Jimenez said, slapping Ashdon on the shoulder, "no hard feelings, right? I should've said something on the drive back. The Harley thing, I mean."

"Uh, well," Ashdon said, "I…I suppose not."

"Dixon *seriously* hates it." He chuckled. "That shit was *hilarious*."

Harland coughed. "All right. Enough—"

Jimenez's walkie-talkie squelched.

"Jesus, are you there?" Cynthia asked, her voice crackling with static. "Over."

Jimenez thumbed the transmit button and acknowledged.

"Have you found Harland yet? Over."

"Yes, ma'am," Jimenez replied. "He's right here. Over."

"Please ask him to report to Security Control Room One immediately. We've got a situation that requires his attention."

Harland dipped his chin. "Tell her I'll be right up."

"He's on his way," Jimenez said. Signing off, he secured his two-way radio. "Damn…must be important."

Harland pulled his beeper from its holder. "She should've just paged me." A blank display greeted him. *Dead?* He tapped the device, then pressed its buttons.

The screen remained dark. *What the hell?*

He returned the pager to his belt. "That's…weird."

"What's wrong?" Jimenez asked.

"My pager's not working."

"Got to be the batteries, right?"

"Yeah," Harland said, "I suppose…they're pretty fresh, though." Jimenez shrugged. "Anyway…I'd better go see what's up." He looked at Ashdon. "You should go to the infirmary. Get checked out. Make sure you don't have a concussion or something."

Ashdon nodded. "That's not a bad idea." He touched a hand to his forehead. "I do feel a bit queasy. Will someone be on duty at this hour, though?"

"Someone's always there," Jimenez said. "People get hurt at *all* hours around here."

"I'm not sure if I'm comforted or—"

"He means," Harland cut in, "because of the late hours people keep. Not because people get hurt a lot…well, not any more than normal…for a place like this."

"Ah, that's a relief…I think." Ashdon stifled a yawn. "Then again…maybe I should just get to bed."

"Get looked at first," Harland said. "You don't want to die in your sleep, do you?"

"Oh, perhaps you're right." Ashdon nodded to Jimenez, then to Harland. "Gentlemen," he said before turning and heading in the direction of the elevators.

"Post a man here to keep watch," Harland said after the scientist had departed, "and contact someone in maintenance. Make sure they're looking into the power failure." He glanced toward the hallway where Ashdon had disappeared. "And make sure that Ashdon gets to the infirmary."

"No problem," Jimenez said. "I'll do it myself." He smirked with a gleam in his eye. "You want me to shoot him if he doesn't go?"

"Yeah," Harland agreed with a snort. "If he's not going to take care of himself, it's probably easier on everyone." He waved a hand. "On second thought…no, don't shoot him. But let me know if he doesn't get there." Harland looked around at the encircling men. "The rest of you— patrol the vicinity." He stabbed a finger at the dais. "If that thing starts lighting up or you see anything or anyone suspicious, notify me immediately." He touched a hand to the dead pager on his belt. "I'm going to find batteries, but if I don't reply within a few minutes of a page, come and find me."

"Sure thing, *jefe*," Jimenez replied, saluting along with the other men.

Harland moved to depart, then stopped short. "Oh, and Jimenez?"

"Yes, sir?"

"Take the friggin' *stairs* if you do."

Chapter 10

Cleansing Fire

Harland found Cynthia talking to Lattimer and Mathis. The trio stared at the monitors but turned as he entered. Even Roberts, still wearing his headphones, appeared distracted from his audio surveillance by the video feeds. Noticing Harland's gaze, the agent looked away, regarding the controls in front of him with exaggerated concentration.

"There you are," Cynthia said. "I tried paging—"

"Batteries are dead." Harland thrust his chin toward the monitors. "What's the situation?"

"See for yourself," she replied, pointing a finger at the screen. "Jason spotted the first one on a perimeter camera."

"The one for the road in," Mathis added, sitting taller in his chair.

Harland stepped closer, squinting at the black-and-white video feed. "I don't see anything."

"It must have moved out of line of sight," Lattimer said. "I can—"

"There," Cynthia hissed, stabbing a finger.

Her gesture was unnecessary—the same movement had already caught Harland's eye. He leaned closer as a blob of illumination moved across the screen. The picture was poor, but the general shape and brightness implied only one thing.

"Damn," Harland muttered. *A fire elemental.* "Is that what I think it is?"

"Another fire entity," Cynthia confirmed.

"Not just one," Lattimer said. "That's the *fifth* one that's crossed the road."

That's a bit too close for comfort, he thought. "Where are they headed?"

"Hard to say," Lattimer said, "but judging by their direction of travel…here."

"Are you sure?" Harland asked. "That's the road in…if they're crossing perpendicular to—"

"The road meanders." Mathis drew an S in the air with his index finger. "They're taking the direct route."

"Right," Harland said. "Good point."

"Guess they're not much for roads…" Lattimer trailed off as another fire elemental drifted into view. "That's six."

"Do we have them on any other cameras?"

"Not yet," Lattimer said. "Not from their direction of approach."

Mathis pointed to another monitor. "That is, not until they get to the parking lot."

"All right," Harland said. "Let's not panic yet. At least not until we know what we're dealing with." He snatched a few walkie-talkies from a nearby table and handed one to Cynthia.

"What's this for?" she asked, holding it by its antenna like a used diaper.

"So I can reach you," Harland replied, adjusting his radio's frequency to match hers. "I'm going to the roof to take a look."

"What should I do?"

"Go wake up Wallace," Harland said, "in case this gets ugly."

Cynthia bit her lip. "If this is nothing, he's *not* going to be happy."

"He'll be even less happy if it turns out to be *something* and we didn't wake him." Harland pulled open the door and looked back. "Besides, you're just the messenger. I'll take full responsibility."

Without another word, he left and hustled for the bank of elevators. The creatures moved fast, so there was no telling how much time he had to gather intel before they did…something. Despite the urgency, the elevator rose at a crawl as if raised by a donkey pulling a rope. Harland wasn't sure if it was a result of his imagination or a consequence of the recent power failure. As thoughts of hitting the emergency stop button and prying open the doors danced through his head, the car finally reached the roof. He exited before the doors had fully opened, ran across the tarmac of the empty helipad, and peered out into the desert to the west. A strong wind blew fresh air, almost chilly at the early hour, across his face as he glanced back to the east. The sun had not yet broken the horizon.

He checked his watch. *Just after five a.m.*

He turned his gaze to the western plain, where the light that heralded the sun's arrival provided some illumination. After his eyes adjusted to the dim light, shrubs, boulders and undulations in the terrain revealed themselves. He saw no fire elementals.

Should've brought binoculars, he thought, squinting. *Wait…there!*

Pinpoints of fiery light danced over the desert floor, chased by near-imperceptible trails of fire. Perhaps ten fire elementals approached. Judging by the lines drawn by their fire trails, they would miss the Institute by a half mile or so.

Good, he thought. *Even if they redirect toward us, we can handle that many.* He thought of the others imprisoned in the depths of the Institute. *A few more for the collection.*

He took a deep breath and expelled it in a rush before raising his two-way radio to his lips. "Cynthia, do you read me? Over."

Several seconds passed, followed by a squelch of noise.

Cynthia's voice came through a moment later, crystal clear. "Here," she said. "How does it look? Over."

The high-powered walkie-talkies had trouble penetrating into the sublevels, so he guessed that she had made her way above ground in the time since he had left her in the security room.

"Not great." He filled her in on what he'd seen. "They might just be passing through, but we'll prep teams to seek and capture…or destroy, if necessary."

"Okay," Cynthia said. "I already woke up Wallace. I'm meeting him in his office. Are you coming down?"

"Negatory," he said, forgetting to wait for her to signal that she'd finished speaking. "I'll coordinate from here and provide overwatch. Over."

"Roger that. I'll notify Wallace. Over."

"Radio if you need me. Dixon out."

"If you're not coming here," he said aloud, "where are you bastards going?"

Is there another dais right in our backyard?

He walked toward the north edge of the roof, where the approaching enemy would pass if they stayed on their current heading.

"Dixon," said Jimenez's voice, broadcast from Harland's two-way. "Do you copy? Over."

"Roger that," he replied. "What's up?"

Harland looked out over the desert.

"You didn't answer your pager. Over."

Empty desert lay to the north.

"Oh, right," Harland said. "Something came up."

There were no daises or notable structures. *Not that I'd see them from here. Besides, they must be hidden like the others or we'd have found them long ago.*

Patting the balustrade that ringed the edge of the roof, he walked east to where the light continued to brighten. To approach the edge on that side, he found it necessary to step over ductwork and piping and slip through a tangle of ventilation and air-conditioning units, the largest of which towered over him.

Pumping clean, radon-free cool air into the depths of the Institute required copious amounts of energy. Though connected to the state's electrical grid, the Institute supplemented its considerable power needs with wind and solar, as well as electrical generators that ran on fossil fuels. This ensured the remote facility could continue to operate even when the power company experienced an outage. Perhaps more importantly, it both cut and hid the cost of cooling the massive facility. The latter being helpful in reducing the likelihood that someone would question why or how a building just a few stories high would have energy needs more appropriate to a Manhattan skyscraper.

"Thought you'd want to know…the new guy, Ashdon. He didn't make it to the infirmary. Over."

"You didn't shoot him, did you? Over."

Something moved in the east. Shading his face with a hand, he squinted into the dawn.

Jimenez chuckled. "Got to find him first. You want me to keep looking? Over."

Sweat broke out on his forehead, despite the cool breeze. He could see them now: more pinpricks of firelight dancing on the plain within the shadow of the hills that lay at their backs.

"Negatory," Harland said. "Forget about that for now. Get up here ASAP and bring an extra assault rifle…and lots of ammo." He filled Jimenez in on the approaching threat.

"Sure, but what's your twenty? Over."

"I'm on the roof," Harland replied. "Now move it. We've got tangos on approach."

"Roger that. Jimenez out."

Lowering the radio, he peered at the approaching points of light. He counted dozens before giving up. It could be described only as an army…or horde.

A phrase came to mind, pulled from some dusty corner of his memory. *For with the dawn rises a cleansing fire, and none shall survive the day of its passage unpurified.* Fitting, even if he couldn't remember the quote's origins.

Harland raised his two-way, already running through scenarios and next steps. Calling back his offsite SRT units would take too long. With a skeleton crew onsite, he'd have no choice but to call for military support. They were closer and had the firepower to deal with an incursion of this scale.

Harland would have preferred to avoid a fight. In his experience, you could often accomplish more with fewer casualties with finesse, subterfuge and diplomacy. Yet there was no time left for finesse or subterfuge, and he doubted diplomacy was an option with this foe. *It'd be like negotiating with a forest fire. At least Wallace won't be chewing my ass for the early wake-up call.*

He spent the next ten minutes on his two-way, radioing his senior officers, passing along his orders and plan of defense. Having done so, he radioed Springer, ordering him to relocate the conference room detainees to the subterranean levels.

He *had* hoped to keep the kids ignorant of the secret underground installation, but he'd deal with *that* problem later. For now, their survival trumped secrecy.

He radioed Cynthia next to update her and Wallace. After Harland had explained the situation, Wallace promised to get on the horn and request armed support from the neighbouring military installation. Scrambling the soldiers and transporting them to the Institute would take time, though. By Harland's estimation, the oncoming horde would arrive first. *We'll just have to hold them off until then.*

The elevator dinged to his right and the doors slid open.

"About time," Harland said, stepping toward it. He stopped in his tracks as Gary Ashdon emerged. "Ashdon, what are you…?"

He trailed off as Jimenez appeared, his assault rifle held at his side, another slung over his shoulder. "Hey, *jefe*. Look who I found on the way here."

Ashdon scratched his neck. "Hey."

"Did you get checked out?" Harland said, knowing the answer.

"Uh, no," Ashdon replied, "I did not…while I appreciate your concern, I felt much better by the time I made it there. I thought perhaps a walk to clear my head—"

"Found him out of breath on the stairs," Jimenez said, holding out the extra assault rifle. "Figured we'd risk the elevator the rest of the way."

"The stairs?" Harland said, taking the proffered weapon. Slinging the M16 over his shoulder, he looked at Ashdon. "Getting some exercise?"

"Indeed," Ashdon said, watching as Jimenez handed Harland a few extra magazines. "Well…after hearing of Mr. Jimenez's misadventure with the elevators, I felt it best to use the stairwells for the time being. At least until the power issues have been investigated and resolved."

"Just like you said, *jefe*." Jimenez tilted his head toward the elevators. "Maintenance says it's all good, by the way."

"Nonetheless," Ashdon continued, "I've had enough

excitement for the day. I was heading to my quarters, but Jesus suggested that I accompany him here." Ashdon raised a brow. "He was quite insistent."

"Holy…" Jimenez's mouth gaped as he looked east. "That's a lot of them."

Harland followed his gaze. "Yeah…won't be long now."

Ashdon swallowed. "Can you handle that many?"

"You should get to the main entrance, Jimenez. Rejoin your team."

Ashdon tented his hands over his eyes, walking northeast, toward the roof's edge. "There must be hundreds…"

"Where do you want us?" Jimenez said, pressing the elevator button. The doors opened immediately.

"Lewis is coordinating defense from there," Harland said. "He'll let you know where he wants you deployed."

Jimenez regarded Harland with wild eyes and smiled. "Time for some fucking payback."

"Just don't get yourself killed," Harland said as the doors began to close.

"Gotta die sometime, *jefe.*"

Chapter 11

Kellerman's Car

Harland joined Ashdon by the roof's edge. The younger man looked out at the approaching menace as if trying to decide whether to order a burger or fries at a fast-food joint.

"There are too many, aren't there?" Ashdon said, keeping his gaze on the plain.

The fire elementals were recognizable now as the monsters that they were, shadowed in their trek by swirling vortices of fire twice their height. They were moving to the west, passing north of the Institute to congregate, facing the facility like soldiers on a battlefield about to storm the walls of a medieval fortress.

Except the Institute isn't *a fortress*, Harland mused. *Just an office building…with far too many glass windows.*

"Military support is en route," Harland answered, raising his walkie-talkie. "We'll have to tough it out until then."

He strode along the roof's edge to the west, issuing orders and gathering and sending intel into the two-way. Ashdon's shuffling footsteps trailed him as he moved.

"Will they be enough?" Ashdon asked with a steady voice. He pointed east. "I see more coming over the hill."

"Beats me," Harland said with a frown. "Probably not." He stopped and looked back at Ashdon. "You should get below ground—to your quarters. Bar the door."

Ashdon glanced toward the elevators. "Shouldn't we

evacuate?"

"There's not enough time," Harland said. "Evacuees would be more at risk out in the open. Even in vehicles, they'd be running the gauntlet, and these things are attracted to movement."

"Perhaps I should stay…to…to help."

Harland smirked. "Can you shoot?"

"Well…no."

Harland waved a hand as if shooing a fly. "Thanks, but don't worry about it. It's my job to protect *you*. You wouldn't want me helping you mix chemicals, would you?"

"Well," Ashdon said with a faint grin, "you did a fine job assisting me with the Winterboy simulacra."

Harland laughed. "I knew I liked you, Ashdon. But seriously, get your ass to safety. Better take the stairs. With everyone scrambling, you might have to wait for an elevator."

Ashdon gave a grim nod. "Very well. Good—"

"Dixon," Lewis said, his voice coming from the walkie-talkie held at Harland's side. "They're coming! Are you seeing this?"

Harland jabbed a finger at the stairwell, then turned and sprinted west. The stairwell door slammed shut as he reached the roof's western edge. *Good man, Ashdon. That's* one *less thing to worry about.*

Countless rivers of flame streaked toward the Institute. From the direction of the rising sun, a sonorous crackling rumble heralded the imminent arrival of the enemy mob. Within minutes, balls of flame would crash against the stone and glass of the Institute. Harland knew from past observation that any that made it through would surely set anything flammable alight.

He spat into his walkie-talkie, verifying his forces were in position. As he'd instructed, they'd spread out to cover the main entryways. Most to the north and west, where the main attack seemed likely to come, and a smaller number to the south and east.

"All right," Harland said. "I see them. Hold your fire. Wait until they're in range."

Though the elementals had not seemed all that intelligent, they'd chosen their side of attack well. The Institute's vulnerable points lay mainly on the north, west, and south sides. The east side, from where the bulk of them had arrived, had reinforced doors and few windows that an enemy could reach.

Special Response Teams—backed by regular security wielding fire suppression equipment—were to engage and slow the enemy, buying time for military support to arrive. They were to stay within the building itself, using it as cover, and defend themselves with heavy weapons, fire extinguishers and water hoses.

Should do about as much good as spitting on a bonfire, but it's all we've got. The fire these beasts hurled seemed to bend the known rules of combustion. While accelerated and intensified by conventional fuel sources, their fires burned and raged even in the absence of any apparent combustible material.

The fire sprinklers will have to do the rest, he thought, struggling to slow his breathing. *Why do they call them* fire *sprinklers when they sprinkle* water? He stifled a manic laugh that morphed into a snarl. *C'mon, Harland, get it together.* He'd seen what fire could do to the human body. He'd heard the screams—years ago in war—and mere hours ago in the desert. *Been too long since I've been in combat.* If there was a worse way to go, he didn't know what it could be. He shuddered and patted the stock of his weapon. *No* way *I'm going out* that *way*.

The first salvo of fireballs arced toward the Institute's

walls. The time for worry and doubt had ended. Gunfire erupted from below him, cutting into the approaching conflagration, a scythe of destruction that slowed and toppled the lead attackers.

Harland punched a fist in the air, watching their molten essence spill onto the earth as those still coming launched a second hell storm at the defenders. Crouching, he rested the muzzle of his M16 on the roof's edge and chose a target, firing controlled bursts until the beast fell, then moved on to another, emptying the magazine.

His accuracy drew unwanted attention.

A rumbling crackle like a thousand hornets in a kettle of popping corn buzzed past his ear. He flinched and back-pedalled as another crashed against the wall in front of him, just below the lip. Catching his foot on something, he stumbled and fell to his back on the layer of gravel that covered much of the roof. Round pebbles dug into his elbows and shoulder blades, but adrenalin dulled the pain.

Harland rolled to his stomach, then army-crawled to the wall's edge, digging a trench through the stones. *That's it for this suit.* He reached for a spare magazine, ripping the pocket that held it as he wrestled it free, before sliding it into place. Preparing to rise, he hesitated, then scuttled sideways several feet before raising his head. *Always keep the enemy guessing about your movements.*

Popping up from cover, he fired again, taking down another. Some of the enemy continued to close the distance to the facility, while others hung back and rained fire at the walls. The sound of shattering glass mingled with weapons fire and screams from below. Whether battle cries of defiance or shouts of pain, Harland could not be certain.

As his second magazine ran dry, Harland heard more yelling from below. Judging by the words, elementals had penetrated into the building proper. He peeked over the edge, despite the risk, as several fire elementals raced from inside hissing and steaming, pursued by the Institute's defenders. Fifty feet from the front entrance, they toppled to the earth. *Fire suppressed, you bastards.*

The thrumming roar of a souped-up V8 engine added to the tumult as a desert-gold sports car shot into view from the north-side parking lot, tearing across the pavement like a bat out of hell.

Is that Kellerman's car? Harland remembered the agent showing it off to the team the day he'd bought it. As far as he knew no one else at the Institute drove one, but the kid should be with his unit, fighting. *What the hell is he doing?!*

The car fishtailed, nearly hitting one of the monsters. A cluster of elementals broke away from a larger mob, flocking to intercept the fleeing vehicle. A line of the invaders formed to the vehicle's front, blocking off its route of escape. Fireballs struck the car from multiple directions as the driver swung it back toward the building.

More elementals bled away from the main horde, revealing a figure at their centre. Clad only in fire and muscled like a bodybuilder, it stood more than seven feet tall, with skin the colour of fresh blood and ember-hot horns blazing like dual torches.

Harland's jaw dropped as recognition dawned. *The figure from the photos.* He raced along the wall, heading for the northwest corner, eyeballing the new arrival the entire way. *Do we need soldiers…or a priest?*

The fiend continued to point, sending elementals in different directions. Some joined the pursuit of the fleeing automobile. Others veered left and right to engage the Institute defenders in the north and south, while the majority drove forward to assault the breach at the main entrance.

Dropping to his knees, he laid his rifle's muzzle on the parapet, took aim and fired. Bullets stitched the ground at the demon's feet before two buried themselves in the thing's leg. The demon snarled as nearby fire elementals threw themselves into the line of fire. Others rushed to join them, swirling about the fire demon, shielding their leader from further attack.

Harland stood to get a better angle and continued to fire into the crowd, aiming for their middle, where he judged that the leader would be. As the gun ran dry, one of their number finally shuddered before toppling to the earth. The rest of the swarm whirled on Harland. With disturbing synchronicity, their fiery hands blurred, winging dozens of flaming projectiles in his direction, chased by shrieks of elemental outrage.

"Oh, shit." Harland dropped to the ground, wincing as pebbles dug into his knees and palms. He rolled to the side. Most of the missiles hit the wall, but a few sailed high. They landed on the roof behind him, where they exploded, charring the gravel before fading to black.

He took a moment to catch his breath, still hearing the chatter of gunfire from his men and screech of Kellerman's tires on the asphalt out front. Tucking his weapon to his side, he army-crawled back from the edge before regaining his feet, hoping he was far enough away that the enemy couldn't target him.

Unless, he thought, wiping sweat from his brow, *they lob them over the rim like Molotov cocktails and get lucky.*

As he lowered his arm, a gust of cold air swept his hair to the side. Glass-hard pellets dusted his cheeks. He ducked his chin and winced as bits of the hard debris flew into his eyes. He raised both hands to shield his face. His cheeks reddened, battered by the wind's bitter chill. He turned his back to the draft and wiped the sand from his face.

Harland looked down at his hands. *No, not sand.* He rolled the particles between his fingertips, feeling them melt under the touch of his body heat. *Ice. What the hell?*

Ice and cold on a warm August morning in the middle of Nevada would have been hard to believe on a normal day. In the midst of an attack by a mob of molten life forms, it couldn't have been more unexpected.

He could only guess that the invaders were somehow the cause. *Are they doing this?* Harland didn't know what to think, but there had to be a connection. It was too much to be a coincidence. *Whatever…that's something for the science teams to figure out later…if they can.*

Still shielding his face against the icy gale, he moved south before edging west toward the melee, keeping low. Ready to retreat if the enemy should target him again, he stood taller and strode forward to reveal himself. *If they're aiming at me, they're not attacking my men.* Able to see more of the plain once again, Harland spun his head to the left, attracted by the movement of incoming armoured personnel carriers, barrelling up from the south. *Not a moment too soon.*

As he scanned the scene, the cold wind continued to blow, tugging at his clothes and extremities. In the distance, beyond the most distant attacker, Kellerman's car coughed and backfired, losing speed. A single tenacious elemental gave solitary pursuit. Even as the vehicle continued to decelerate, the last pursuer finally abandoned the chase, turning back to join its fellows in assaulting the Institute. Then, the engine revved, tires squealed, and the car shot forward once again in a cloud of black exhaust.

The air slowed a moment later, as if someone had flipped the off switch on a wind machine. He rubbed feeling back into his cheeks, then held out a hand. Fluffy white snowflakes landed in his palm, flashing iridescent in the morning light before dissolving a second later.

Drying his hand on his blazer, he looked again for Kellerman's car. Through a veil of falling snow, he watched as the gold-coloured muscle car continued to speed away to safety, having somehow run the gauntlet and survived.

At least someone's going to make it through this, Harland thought as the car faded into the distance. *Can't really blame you for running, Kellerman, but if I make it out of this…your ass is fired!*

Chapter 12

Dragoons and Fire

No longer distracted by the fleeing vehicle, the elemental invaders moved toward the breach once again, hissing angrily beneath the sudden snowstorm. As they did so, soldiers disembarked from personnel carriers to the left, followed by a number of light tanks. The former opened fire and moved north to sandwich the enemy between themselves and the Institute. Armoured fighting vehicles—Dragoons, judging by their outlines—sped to their front, providing cover against attack, even as their weapons ports spat ammunition at the attackers. In response, a legion of elementals charged the soldiers, zigzagging in their approach, hurling fire, while another group stormed into the Institute.

The tanks were currently near useless on both fronts. One battlefront lay too close to the soldiers, the other too close to the Institute. Firing their main guns at either risked doing more harm than good, at least for now. However, they did serve as mobile cover, and if the elementals should choose to flee, the tanks would no doubt make them regret it.

"Lewis," Harland shouted into his walkie-talkie. "Report. Can you hold? Over."

Seconds passed with no reply.

"Negative," Lewis said finally. "Sprinklers cut out. The atrium's soaked. That's all that's holding them back. Just me and the fire crew now."

"How long can you hold?" Harland stuck his head over the lip of the wall. At the centre of a huddle of elementals, the fire demon moved its hands like a martial artist practising slow-motion katas. Distracted, he missed Lewis's response. "Say again?"

"A couple minutes."

Flames formed at the demon's feet, swirling like a dust devil, then took off toward the main entrance like a dog chasing a squirrel.

"Things are drying up faster than—"

"Do your best," Harland said, wide-eyed as he watched the mini-cyclone's approach. "Retreat if you *have* to. I'm coming down."

The swirl of flame grew steadily larger as it thundered toward him. Easily sixty feet high and thirty in diameter, its rate of growth accelerating.

Transfixed by the sight, Harland stumbled back, catching his feet on the lip of the helipad. He toppled, jarring his wrists on the asphalt. He rubbed his battered palms against his chest and looked up at the apex of the tornado of fire—now fifty feet higher than the roof on which he sat—as it swirled ever faster and rammed the front of the Institute. Glass and other debris tore from the facade, creating deadly projectiles, as the twister ripped into the building.

Harland crab-walked away from the storm, turning his face from the stifling heat. Flipping onto his stomach, he pushed himself to his feet and raced for the stairs. Nearly out of ammo and with the enemy so close, he couldn't do much more up here. He'd have to descend to the first floor and join the fight there.

He wrenched the door open and plunged inside, chased by the ear-splitting shriek of sundered metal coming from the Institute's main entrance. Gripping the door by its edge, he tugged against the hydraulic spring, failing to hasten the door's closure by more than a few milliseconds.

Grasping the handrail for support, he sank into a crouch, resting his rear on the top step.

"Dixon," said Lewis over the radio. "You there?"

"I'm here."

"We lost the atrium," Lewis said. "Some kind of fire twister lit us up. Hostiles have entered the facility."

"I know," Harland said. "I saw."

"We had to retreat," Lewis added. "Sorry, Dixon."

"Don't sweat it." Harland dragged himself upright. "Withdrawing was the right move." He looked at the stairwell door. "I had to do it myself."

"I think I lost my eyebrows," Lewis said absently. "I can't feel 'em."

Harland turned and began to descend. "Where are you now?"

"Stairwell A," replied Lewis. "We wedged the door, but they're trying to break it down. These fuckers are *strong*. Not sure it'll hold."

"Okay," Harland said. "Non-combatants are holed up on sublevels eight, nine and ten. Spread your men across those levels. Watch the doors and seal any breaches with extreme prejudice."

"They're all down," Lewis said. He sounded out of breath, with a slight hitch to his speech, as if jogging. "It's just me and a few from the fire crew now."

"Shit," Harland muttered. He drew to a halt and grimaced at the radio, resisting the urge to hurl it against the stone wall below. "Acknowledged." He drew a deep breath before continuing. "Do your best. Get the academics to help with defense."

"If they make it through the doors," Lewis said, "I don't

think we can hold them…at least not for long. Not with just me, a fire crew, and a bunch of—"

"Understood," Harland replied, "but maybe these bastards won't find you for a while. Doors below ground are all locked and reinforced and these things don't have access cards. Just make sure to stay quiet. We've just got to hold out while the cavalry helps us regain control."

"What's their endgame, Dixon? Are they after their buddies in the holding cells? Some kind of revenge? Over."

"How the hell should I know?" Harland said. He resumed his descent, bounding down the stairs, taking them two at a time. "Sorry, Lewis. That's not a bad guess, but they already lost more than that getting this far." He paused, pondering the question more deeply. "It's got to be the dais, same as the other incursions."

"If you're right," Lewis said, "then they may not be after us. We might just be in their way."

"Exactly," Harland said. "So keep your heads down. I don't want to lose anyone else."

"What are you gonna do?"

"Gather some intel," Harland replied. "Maybe see if I can communicate with their leader."

"Are you sure that's wise? The big guy doesn't seem like much of a talker."

"Probably not…but somebody's got to do it. Good luck. Dixon out."

Reaching the main floor, he burst out into the hall and turned left, working his way to the front of the building. Shooting guns and the susurration of fire and falling debris played backup band to a rhythmic thumping like the drums of war. Even if he hadn't already known the building's layout intimately, the noise would have served as a guide. When he got to the hallway leading to the atrium itself, he paused by the corner and peered around its edge.

A group of elementals crowded by the entrance to Stairwell A. The largest one pounded huge dents into the door, softening the metal beneath the heat of its fists like a blacksmith working a sword. If the door hadn't been reinforced and fireproofed, they'd likely have already broken through.

Harland resisted the urge to open fire.

There were too many to fight and every moment the door delayed the elementals improved the Institute's chances. Shooting the guy beating on the door wouldn't help either; another would take his place.

No…better to gather intel…and wait for backup. As he made that decision, flaming horns appeared at the far side of the mob. Moving above the assembly like the sails of a ship, they came closer, parting the throng.

As the scarlet-skinned giant finally emerged from the crowd, the lead elemental bowed and sidestepped, clearing a path for its master. On uninjured legs, the demon squared off with the blackened and dented stairwell door.

No…fucking…way. He'd seen the bullets hit, heard the shout of pain. *You can't possibly have healed that fast.*

Touching both hands to the barrier, the thing pushed. Moments later, the door bent inward, twisting in the frame, then gave way, collapsing with a crash. With a rumble of satisfaction, the red giant sidestepped, allowing its honour guard to precede it down the stairs.

Harland pulled back behind the corner fully, not wanting to risk being spotted. Even with only his left eye visible, an unlucky glance could bring his foes down upon him.

He leaned against the wall and smiled grimly. There were more enemies than bullets in his gun, but that didn't matter if he could take out their leader. *Cut off the head, the snake will die.* He checked his weapon, counted to five, then looked again. He just had to wait for the right moment.

He didn't have to wait long.

As the last elemental entered the stairwell, Harland stepped out. Pounding his gun's trigger like it owed him money, he sent a hail of lead down the hall. The first few ripped up only drywall, but he used them as a guide to correct his aim. His last two struck the brute in the shoulder. The beast snarled and grabbed the wall, sending fire along its surface from the point of contact. Snaking for Harland as if alive, it expanded to fill the passageway as it travelled.

With a yelp, he ducked behind the corner, letting the fire blow past. It quickly expended itself but still succeeded in igniting the ceiling before dying away. Residual moisture left by the depleted sprinklers snuffed the ceiling flames moments later.

With the air drying up fast, any new fires were likely to burn unabated. He had to hope that Institute firefighters still roamed the halls and would keep any such blazes from burning entirely out of control. But as long as the enemy walked the Institute's halls, they'd be bailing water out of a leaky boat. The enemy needed to be stopped or the entire building might be lost, along with everyone still in it.

He drew his pistol and reloaded. Counting to five, he emerged from cover with his finger tight against the weapon's trigger.

The fire demon was gone.

Must have followed the others. Determined to catch up, he ran for the stairwell door. With the thing's rear unguarded, he might have a clear shot.

He drew up short at the door's edge and peered inside. Having verified that the demon did not lie in wait, he stepped through the portal, turning sideways to edge past the still-hot metal.

Sweeping ash and cinders from his shoulders, he regarded the depths. The sounds of movement echoed from far below. Harland huffed and puffed, then slapped his cheeks. *Let's do this*, he thought, as he finally began to descend.

With each level, he increased the speed of his descent, hugging the outer wall to avoid the still-burning but dwindling fire trails left by the elementals that had passed before him.

He braced himself as he reached the last landing before sublevel eight—the first of the levels where the PhDs and other non-combatants had sequestered themselves—praying that his foes had continued past.

Having seen the demon crash through the first-floor door like a seven-foot-tall pitcher of Kool-Aid, he'd had to adjust his estimates of how long they could hold out. If they were here for revenge, as Lewis had hypothesized, the losses to the Group could be devastating. Not only in lives, but in the brilliance, expertise and experience of the scientists, engineers, programmers and other academics that would be among the dead. He took some solace in the knowledge that the archival vault door would have sealed itself by now, ensuring that the Institute's priceless assets would survive. Even if they all died here today, the Group would still be able to rebuild and continue its work.

Rounding the corner, he let out the breath he'd been holding. The door leading to sublevel eight remained sealed tight and unmarred.

He relaxed further, seeing the next two levels were likewise undisturbed. Nodding to himself, he resumed his descent. Within a few steps, a thunderous boom reverberated from deeper within the Institute. Harland flinched and stuck his gun out before him, a ward against whatever dwelled below.

With the Institute's people safe, he considered returning to the surface. *What's the point of dying down here?*

He paused, tilting an ear toward the depths. *Because no*

one—not even the devil himself—gets to mess with my people, burn my building, and just walk away.

The sound of tearing metal rang out moments later, followed by bestial roars. Roars that Harland now associated with the invaders when struck by bullets or otherwise in pain. He'd not heard the rhythmic pop of an M16, so if members of his team had engaged the enemy, they were using something other than guns. *Probably fire extinguishers or hoses.* Whoever it was, they needed his help. *Nice not to be alone down here, at least.*

Placing his feet with care, Harland forced himself deeper into the depths as the clatter below grew fainter.

His guess that the horde had come for the dais became a certainty as he reached subfloor fifteen. The metal door had been shoved inward, ripped from its frame along with chunks of concrete. It lay on the far side of the hall, half-buried in wallboard. Fire elemental remains dotted the floor; blackened islands of ash encircled by a thin flood of water. As he stood there and scanned for threats, that same water spread past Harland's feet, scurrying into the stairwell before cascading down the steps.

Chapter 13

Enter the Insect

Looking up, he saw why. The pipe that supplied water to the fire sprinklers—presumably from a different source than the main floor's atrium—jutted down from the ceiling, torn from its moorings and pinched and rolled shut as if in a massive vise.

Lewis was right. *These bastards* are *strong.*

Of course, it wasn't a perfect seal. The water that merely dribbled from it told Harland that much of the supply had been spent. No doubt most of what had fallen had already poured down the stairs to lower levels or spread into nearby rooms.

Beyond the water's edge, the hallway leading toward the Agora lay in ruins. Streaks of fire still burned upon the floor, filling the air with noxious fumes. Posters and bulletin boards burned on the walls, and clouds of dark smoke gathered by the ceiling.

He'd expected worse. *The sprinklers must have wet the area before the big guy disabled them*, he thought, holstering his pistol. *Good thing, or we'd have a full-scale fire on our hands.*

Knowing that it might not last, Harland tore a fire extinguisher from the wall near the elevators. He took a moment to prime it, then made his way down the smoke-filled corridor in a half-crouch, dousing the surviving flames before they could grow into an uncontrollable blaze.

Before long, his chest ached and his lungs willed him to

breathe, to expel the last fresh breath that he'd taken before entering the smoke.

Feeling red-faced and dizzy, he dropped to the floor and panted like a blacksmith's bellows. Stars clouded his eyes. The air, though clearer near the floor, still threatened to asphyxiate him.

Got to put it out. He coughed and spat. *Give the ventilation system a chance to clear it.*

Taking a deep breath, he pushed himself back to a half-crouch. With a snarl of defiance, he resumed his work, sending puffs of fire retardant left, right, and overhead. With each blast, the air seemed easier to breathe. Not about to give the flames a chance to recover, he kept working the extinguisher until it ran dry.

He tossed it to the side and looked around.

There, he thought, spotting another red canister hanging nearby.

Grabbing it, he continued his trek.

With every step, Harland considered turning tail, but he kept at it—whether out of duty or stubbornness, he wasn't sure. Even staying low, the smoke still drew tears from his eyes. As his stamina started to flag, he spotted a water fountain. He leaned over it to splash his face, clearing the soot and grime, then slurped water. He swished cool liquid between his teeth, spat it out, then drank his fill. Drying his face with a sleeve, he soldiered on, continuing to douse errant flames before they could take hold and grow out of control.

Then, as the extinguisher grew light in his hands, the fires finally relented. He had no trouble determining why. Sprinklers overhead, presumably fed by a different source than those by the stairwell, continued to rain moisture down upon the walls and floor, drenching every surface beyond any chance of fire.

Sagging with relief, he tossed the voided container to the side. Knowing their sensitivity to water, he scanned the floor for signs of fallen elementals. After a moment, he smiled, spotting the telltale charred residue with orangey-red crystalline centre in several places ahead. Not knowing how many had preceded him down the stairs, he couldn't be sure if any had survived the deluge, but he'd take whatever he could get. Either way, he didn't see their monstrous leader among the fallen, and he doubted the beast would be downed so easily.

Harland drew his weapon, hunched his shoulders and plunged into the deluge, able to hear little over its waterfall-like patter and the still-ringing alarm. He soon shivered and his shoes squished, expelling jets of water with each step. His dress shirt clung to his body and water ran down the sides of his face, behind his ears and down his back.

As he neared the Agora, reddish light beckoned from farther down the hall—a lighthouse cautioning him against proceeding further. Heeding its warning, Harland swung to his left.

Too quickly.

His arms flailed as his feet slid from beneath him. His left hip and buttock bashed against the slick floor with a thump as his teeth sank into his tongue.

He pushed himself to his feet with a groan.

Damn, that smarts.

Rubbing his side, he hobbled forward.

As the pain faded to a dull ache, he finally sighted his goal: a red door adorned with red-and-white symbols. He slipped inside, snugging the door shut behind himself. Without pause, he snatched open the door of one of the steel lockers that lined the opposite wall—each the size of a department store change room. A fire proximity suit hung within.

Shivering, he stepped inside.

Fireproof, the room had no sprinklers, and he wel-comed the respite from the downpour in the hall.

Maybe I should get out of these wet clothes first…no…no time, he thought, kicking his sopping dress shoes to the side. He wiggled into loose-fitting silver pants and slid his feet into a pair of heavy-duty fireproof boots. They were a size too large but should stay on his feet, if he didn't try to play basketball in them. He shrugged on the jacket, pulled on gloves and donned the hood before re-entering the hallway.

A shower still fell as he rushed for the Agora. The mois-ture in the air and Harland's sweat, wet hair and respiration soon fogged the gold-plated visor, clouding his vision. He slipped a hand beneath the hood to clear the viewport. When it clouded over a second time, he raised the helmet over his head, using it to deflect the cascade. Able to see clearly again, he moved on.

Twenty feet from the Agora, a voice boomed in his ears, with a clarity and strength that seemed impossible in the midst of the cacophony that enveloped him. Incompre-hensible, guttural snarling, akin to a tiger with a head cold hacking up phlegm and gargling it, punctuated by incon-gruous sibilant hisses. It was a language no human being could hope to utter.

Harland's heart thumped as a chill ran through him that had little to do with the damp clothes beneath his fire suit. In spite of the churn in his guts, he stole closer and looked within, not daring to breathe.

The fire demon and three elementals congregated near the Agora's epicentre, sheltered within a swirling nimbus of pulsating fire eighty feet in diameter. The aura of fire hissed and spat with every drop from the sprinklers, high overhead—at least those droplets that did not evaporate in the heat before reaching its roiling perimeter.

Pieces of the booth that had housed the dais lay strewn against the far wall. The dais that it had formerly contained lay at the demon's feet, near the Agora's centre, its unnatural glow scarcely visible against the intensity of the firelight. The demon and its surviving minions had their backs to him, eyes fixated on the white globe of energy floating above the dais. As with the one at Alpha site, this orb shone with an inner light brighter than that of the blaze surrounding it.

Scuttling inside, Harland took shelter behind a pillar as wide as a sequoia tree and peered around its side. He lowered the hood of his fire suit back into position and patted down the cowl. Water drizzled against the hood, still falling unhindered at his position beyond the fire maelstrom's edge. He shook off a glove and reached under the hood's lip a moment later. After several tries, his fingers closed on the protective jacket's zipper. Slipping a hand inside, he dug out his pistol, palmed it with his still-gloved hand, and zipped himself back up. The thick padding of the suit's protective gauntlet precluded the possibility of firing his weapon while wearing them, so he left it where it lay.

Before the visor could cloud again, he stepped out and raised his pistol, holding his gloved hand against his gun-hand wrist to steady it. *Say hi to the devil for me.*

As he squeezed the trigger, the remaining elementals threw themselves into the line of fire, shielding their leader from harm. They had heard him, somehow, despite the clamour of fire and rain. He kept firing, content to settle for a lesser target. The closest elemental staggered and slowed as Harland's bullets punched holes through its torso. The two behind it fanned left and right. Drawing parallel with their injured comrade, they raised their arms to return fire.

Seeing the danger, Harland turned to flee. Twin

impacts—one between his shoulder blades, the other in the back of his neck—knocked the air from his lungs and bruised his spine. The fire suit kept the balls from burning holes in his back, but it still felt like getting pummelled with baseballs shot from a cannon. He dove forward and rolled to his right. More incendiaries struck the floor to his left. The evasive manoeuvre had worked, but he knew that more would soon follow. He scootched to his right, avoiding another flaming projectile before making it back to the dubious safety of the pillar.

He huddled in the shadow of the concrete support, weapon clutched against his chest, and assessed his limited options. If he'd counted right, he had just two rounds left. He had more in his suit pocket, but they'd be on him before he got the zipper down. Resigned, he turned to fire his last rounds and go down fighting. Before he could do so, familiar roars echoed off the walls. He glanced back through the fogging visor, keeping his gun at the ready but holding fire. The trio hovered at the edge of the firestorm, eyeing the still-falling water with rage-filled eyes.

Thank God, he thought, fighting with his zipper to gain access to his suit jacket and the ammunition within. *Just need to reload.*

The drumming of water on his hood eased as he dropped his pistol's near-empty clip to the floor.

C'mon, c'mon.

He fumbled the fresh one into place.

Yes!

Then the water stopped entirely.

Shit.

The elementals keened in triumph.

Harland scurried to the other side of the pillar. Getting a clear shot and taking down the leader was his only hope against these odds. A Hail Mary pass. Just like in his high school quarterbacking days. Always risky, but he had little to lose. Even with the fire suit, his odds of surviving five minutes against these things weren't good.

Harland looked to the ceiling. *Is this it?* He'd fought the good fight many times before, putting his life on the line for his country. He'd accepted the risks and knew that you couldn't keep rolling those dice and expect to keep winning. No matter how lucky you are, eventually they're going to come up snake eyes. If his time had finally come, he wasn't going to cry about it now. Besides, he'd had a good run…made it further than he'd expected. *I could be a grandfather, for Pete's sake.* It was a fact he'd usually thrust to the back of his mind—preferring to bury the unpleasant calculus of mortality in the distractions of a busy life—but it comforted him now.

Then again, he wasn't going to lie down and die either. He wanted to live. To survive. If he could. Not for the first time, he considered making a run for it, but he'd seen how fast these things could move—he couldn't outrun them. However, the suit might allow him to survive long enough to get away. That is, if they chose to pursue him. Until he'd arrived, they seemed more interested in the dais, so maybe they'd let him go. He could head for the surface and come back with an army. Except that would take time. *Giving this guy time to do whatever he's trying to do.* And whatever that was, he had a feeling it wasn't good. Some instinct told him that it was true.

He pushed himself to his feet, panic giving way to calm resignation.

"*Intra, insectum,*" said the fire demon, loud enough to be heard even over the raging firestorm.

Is that Latin? The harsh, guttural voice and Harland's lack of skill with the language, made it hard to tell. *Enter, insect?*

Another voice rose above the gale in reply.

"I don't know what you think you're doing," shouted the voice, "but I think you should go!"

Ashdon?

Chapter 14

Go Back, Satan

K neeling, Harland braced himself against the column and peered out at the scene. The three elementals buzzed about the demon like bees around a hive. They kept watchful eyes on Ashdon as they did so, no doubt ready to throw themselves into danger to protect their master, as they had during Harland's first assassination attempt.

The demon laughed and gargled a reply. Most words were unintelligible, but *mori* stood out.

Die, Harland translated after a moment's thought. *No shit. He's not even wearing a fire suit.* That Ashdon was not yet a pile of ash seemed a miracle. He could only guess that the intruders were confused by the inexplicable show of defiance. *Like a rabbit snarling at a cougar instead of running for its life.*

"Ashdon," Harland muttered under his breath, "you crazy bastard. What are you doing?"

"Oh," Ashdon said to the fiend. "I see." He cleared his throat. "*Loquerisne anglice?*" The demon tilted its head. "No…I imagine not." Ashdon unleashed another stream of Latin, too fast for Harland to catch more than a few words.

Non nocere? *Do no harm? Is he reciting the Hippocratic Oath?*

Harland leaned left, peering around the pillar's edge. Thick condensation coated his helmet's visor, giving it all the transparency of a frost-coated window. Ashdon was a smudge on the left; the elementals, orangey-red blobs on the right within an enclosing bubble of flickering luminosity.

How is he still alive? Any surprise the creatures felt over Ashdon's sudden appearance should have passed by now, yet they just stood there. Stood there, while he spoke to them like teenagers he'd caught egging his car. *It's not mercy; not from these things.* They had invaded with pitiless ferocity, immolating countless Institute defenders without hesitation or regret. Yet despite Ashdon having interrupted their ritual, neither the demon nor its allies had attacked him. More than that, the fiend had deigned to converse, while eyeing the defenseless biochemist with an almost wary expression. *Is that the key? That he's defenseless? Or his command of Latin? Charming personality?* Whatever the reason, the demon's snarl signalled that its patience would soon run out. He needed to act before that happened. When it was just him, he was prepared to go down fighting, but duty demanded that he now get Ashdon clear.

Harland ripped off the hood, tossed it behind the pillar, and sidled to the left, exposing his entire body to the enemy. The demon's head snapped to regard him. Its minions, however, kept their eyes fixed on Ashdon. Able to see properly now, he pointed the muzzle of his pistol between the thing's blazing horns and pulled the trigger.

The creature blurred as the hammer fell, moving faster than Harland could follow. One moment it stood in the centre of the hall, the next it loomed over Ashdon, ten feet beyond the fire bubble's outer edge. Thick fingers coiled around the kid's meagre bicep and lifted him. Ashdon twisted in its grasp but remained trapped. Still holding the scientist in an iron grip, the demon turned, heading back toward the blaze, this time at a leisurely pace.

Realizing that within a few steps, Ashdon would burn, Harland stepped forward. Still aiming his pistol at the demon, he held out his other hand in supplication. "Whoa, whoa," he said. "Easy now. Put him down."

Ashdon twisted to face his captor. With a grunt, he reached up to clutch the thing's wrist with his free hand. Legs dangling, the kid pulled at the beast's arm, as if climbing a tree. "I don't think he understands, Harland."

"*Si* Ashdon *mori*," Harland said, making a downward motion with his free hand, "*tu mori. Vade retro, Satana.*"

"Yes," Ashdon said, wincing as his lab coat began to smoke beneath the demon's touch. "Go back, Satan…or whatever your name is." Ashdon yelped as the demon shook him. "*Vade retro, Satana*," Ashdon spat. The demon's arm brightened as if lit from beneath its scarlet skin. The kid's lab coat began to smoke as arcs of electricity danced along the demon's arm from its wrist to its shoulder. "*Non omnis moriar…*"

Not dying? Harland thought. *That's the spirit, kid.*

Ashdon's lips continued to move, saying something too faint to hear. *Probably wouldn't understand it anyway*, Harland thought, stepping closer. The demon curled its lip and gave a low growl in reply. Ashdon spoke again, his utterance still lost in the roar of fire and arcs of electricity.

The demon's eyes narrowed. It rumbled unintelligibly, as if to itself. "*Volo sed non fugio*," it said finally. *I fly but do not flee*, Harland translated, surprising himself with the abrupt realization. Stimulated by adrenalin, his brain continued to reawaken his dormant Latin, motivated by his desperate need for intel.

The demon spun in a circle, swinging Ashdon like a father giving a child an airplane ride. Twirling a full three hundred and sixty degrees, it let go, launching Ashdon headfirst toward Harland. As he flew, the scientist-turned-missile curled into a ball, striking the ground shoulders first and rolling. The bruises on Harland's back ached in sympathy at the impact.

Slapping the rock-hard tile, the scientist continued through a full somersault and regained his feet, seemingly unharmed and unruffled. Only the blackened arm of his lab coat gave clear evidence of his near-fatal encounter. He'd even managed to keep his eyeglasses, somehow, and pushed them back into place as they teetered at the tip of his nose.

Harland waved Ashdon to his rear and began backing away.

Barking a disdainful farewell, the demon flicked a hand and turned, squaring off with the dais once more as the elementals moved to shield their commander's posterior.

Then the air between them rippled.

He squinted. "What the hell?"

A desert plain, devoid of vegetation, lay in the distance, obscured but not entirely occluded by the walls of the Agora and rooms and hallways that lay beyond them. Lifeless and alien, even with most details lost in the haze of the swirling maelstrom, he knew that it couldn't be the desert outside. That desert lay over a dozen stories above. Only solid earth lay beyond the exterior walls of the facility at this depth.

Harland blinked. *Still there.*

"Come on!" Ashdon said, pulling on Harland's shoulder. "Let's go. Before he changes his mind." Harland's fingers tightened on the grip of his weapon. *Just one lucky shot,* he thought. "Don't do it. You can't win this fight. You're not even in the same *league.*"

Harland pursed his lips and scowled, moving his head side to side. "Fuck." He stabbed a finger at his fiery foes. "This is *not* over."

They gave no sign of having heard him as he sidled to the right, interposing the pillar between himself and the enemy. To his relief, the pillar on this side remained opaque. He finally lowered his weapon, unzipping his suit to return it to its holster.

He turned to Ashdon, who gestured toward the hallway like a movie theatre usher directing traffic. Together they fled down the hallway, shoulder to shoulder, as the firelight at their backs grew brighter. Fifty feet down the hallway, the fluorescent bulbs overhead popped, showering them with glass, and went out. They weren't plunged into complete darkness, though, as twenty feet further along, the lights still shone.

Must be a short. All this moisture can't be good for the wiring.

Thoughts of the electrical system were shoved aside as his companion stumbled.

Harland reached for the other man's elbow. "Hey, buddy! You okay?"

The kid grabbed the wall, then collapsed to the floor.

Harland dropped to his knees. "Ashdon!" He fumbled for Ashdon's wrist. "What's wrong?" *He must have hit his head when that thing tossed him…or the flash of light triggered another epileptic fit.* He expelled a jet of air as his fingers found a pulse. He patted a hand against Ashdon's cheek with increasing force. "C'mon, man."

Ashdon didn't move.

Chapter 15

Fire Escape

Harland grabbed the kid's wrist and pulled, feeling a twinge and rush of warmth in his lower back that he tried to ignore. Heaving, he pulled Ashdon into a fireman's carry. Groaning under the weight, he adjusted the load, trying to get Ashdon's belt buckle to stop digging into his neck. Failing in the attempt, he gave up and trudged for the stairwell.

Sweat soon poured down his face in the unventilated fire suit and his legs burned, but he pushed on, determined to make it as far as the stairwell before taking a rest. As he neared his destination, footfalls pounded down the steps. Jimenez and Springer appeared, breathing heavily, followed by Carlson, a broad-shouldered twenty-something kid.

"Dixon," Jimenez said. "You okay?" Before receiving an answer, the agent shifted his gaze to the man across Harland's shoulders. "Who's that?"

"The new guy," Harland said, dropping the unconscious man's feet to the floor. "Ashdon."

"What happened to him?"

"I think he hit his head," Harland replied. "Here, take him." He held the scientist out toward Jimenez. "Get him to the infirmary."

"Sure thing, *jefe*." Jimenez grabbed Ashdon beneath his armpits and waltzed him in a semicircle, passing him to Carlson.

"Got him," Carlson said, scooping the unconscious man up and across his shoulders with nary a grunt.

"Give me your weapon," Harland said as Carlson turned to leave. "Be gentle," he shouted at Carlson's back as the security operative began to ascend. "See that he's well cared for. He's got more *guts* than sense."

Jimenez eyed Harland. "Are you hurt?"

Harland shook his head. "Nothing that can't wait." He checked the M16 that he'd taken from the departed SRT member, scowling at the half-empty magazine. *It'll have to do.* "Where's our military support?"

"Mopping up topside," Jimenez said. "Lewis is coordinating."

Springer snorted. "Right. More like arguing with their CO."

"What about?"

Springer shrugged. "They were trying to come below ground."

"He sent us down," Jimenez added. "While they figure out who's got security clearance."

Springer looked up. "Lewis has guards posted, just in case."

"Good man," Harland said. "We'll deal with that later." He spun about, beckoning them to follow. "C'mon."

"Where to, *jefe*?"

"The Agora. We've got trespassers to exorcise, including that seven-foot-tall *mutant* leading them."

He filled Jimenez and Springer in on the situation as they strode down the corridor. They kept their weapons raised, ready to shoot anything that moved. The air stank of soot, so humid from the recent deluge that a thin mist drifted a foot above the still-wet floor.

"What's the situation at ground level?" Harland asked.

"Under control," Springer replied. "Gunships and tanks

are chasing down the survivors."

"What about the fires?"

Jimenez grunted. "Fire brigades are doing what they can."

Harland frowned. "Bad?"

"Under…control," Jimenez said, making a face like he'd just bitten into an onion. "Floors above ground are definitely going to need a few coats of paint."

"Looks like it's been napalmed," Springer said, "but the building's intact, structurally at least."

Harland stopped to regard his companions. "Casualties?"

"Dunno." Jimenez studied his feet. "It's not good."

Harland turned to the other man. "What about the detainees?"

Springer rubbed his neck. "Yeah, about that…"

Harland tensed. If they'd been hurt, there'd be a *shitstorm* of trouble coming his way.

"Watch out!" Jimenez shouted.

Harland's head snapped backward as Jimenez yanked on his arm and Springer shoved him in the chest. Stumbling back, he glimpsed a wave of fire swelling toward them from down the hall. The trio crashed to the floor of the lab on the far side of the doorway as flames engulfed the corridor.

Two or three seconds later—though it seemed longer—the fire dissipated, leaving only heat behind.

"All right," Harland said, wriggling out from under the dog pile. "Let me up, dammit."

"Sorry, Dixon," Springer said, extending a hand. Harland clasped it and regained his feet. "Didn't hurt you, did we?"

"Not at all," Harland answered, knuckling his back. "My granny tackles harder than you."

"Your granny's still alive? She must be a *hundred*."

"Ninety-four, actually," Harland replied. "But, dead or alive, my point still stands."

"Nothing broken?" Jimenez asked.

"Why would there be?"

Jimenez shrugged. "Well…you know."

"Know what?"

Jimenez looked at Springer.

"He's worried your old bones can't take a hit," Springer said with a glint in his eye.

Harland scoffed. "Oh, you're going to pay for that one, Springer." He thrust a finger toward the hallway. "I'll show you who's old. Let's move!"

They filed back into the hallway single file. To Harland's relief, the blast had failed to reignite the still-wet corridor. He'd feared they'd be busy putting out fires instead of returning to the Agora, giving their foes more time to complete whatever they were attempting to do with the dais. The wave of fire that had nearly immolated them might be just a taste of whatever was to come, so they needed to be quick.

Gun-shy after the near-miss, they stayed close to the walls and rushed from doorway to doorway. At the first sign of brightening light, they planned to seek shelter in a nearby room. They had no plan for what they'd do if they got caught at the halfway point, other than stop, drop and roll. *And most likely burn*, he thought. They were lucky, though. Another wave of fire did not materialize, and they proceeded the rest of the way unhindered and unharmed.

They burst into the Agora, advancing in a leapfrog pattern—two providing overwatch as the third advanced, but the demon and its minions were nowhere to be seen. Only the sound of dripping water, fluorescent lights and humming ventilation disturbed the calm.

He should have been relieved to find the room empty. To avoid a fight that he wasn't sure that he could win, even with the help of his two armed companions. Yet he couldn't relax until he'd confirmed that the intruders were truly gone…and if they were, that left disturbing questions, such as where they'd escaped to and how.

Harland knew that the daises were involved somehow. They'd been at the site of most incursions, and the demon had been doing something with it when he had first caught up with them here. He thought back to the apparition of the unknown desert, dotted with volcanoes. *Is it the platforms that allow them to appear and disappear?*

Harland scanned the floor. "Where is it?" he asked. "Do you see it?"

"See what, *jefe?*"

"The dais." Harland pointed at the spot where he'd last seen it. "It was right there."

"Dunno," Jimenez said. "Too warm in here, maybe?"

"Yeah, could be," Harland muttered. "We'll have to get some techs in here to check."

He hoped it was gone. If the platforms had allowed the invaders to disappear, it might also allow them to reappear…and maybe bring reinforcements. Either way, he wasn't going to take any chances. If the scientists managed to relocate it, he'd have it moved to one of the holding cells and post round-the-clock guards.

"What do we do now?" Springer asked.

"Search the building," Harland replied. "Top to bottom. Let's make sure they're truly gone."

They combed the immediate area, looking for any sign of the monsters or clues as to where they might have gone. Searching a large, open space like the Agora didn't take long, but they still came up empty. They were preparing to widen their search to the entire floor when a dozen members of Harland's security force arrived. He ordered the new arrivals to assist in the hunt. It wasn't long before someone discovered that the elementals interred down the hall from the Agora had also vanished. Swearing at the news, he instructed everyone to keep at it until they had searched every room, corridor and closet in the building.

It took hours.

When his agents failed to find anything else, the knot in his gut started to loosen at last. He didn't know quite how, but somehow, the fire demon, its minions, and even the dais that seemed to have drawn them to the Institute were gone. Only a trail of destruction, littered with the fallen on both sides, remained to mark their passage.

Chapter 16

Phantom Frost

Harland rubbed his eyes and yawned. After they'd confirmed that the demon and elementals were nowhere to be found, he'd stumbled to his office and collapsed, catching a few, but not nearly enough, much-needed winks on the couch in his office. Having just been awakened by Cynthia, he still struggled to clear the cobwebs from his mind.

"Gone?" he said. "Are you sure?"

"They fled before Springer got to them," Cynthia replied with a nod. "Shattered the door. Looks like they used a chair."

"You're kidding," Harland said. "That's bulletproof glass. And you're sure they're not in the infirmary or something?"

She gave her head a shake. "I verified it myself. I checked the infirmary *and* the gym. They're sending the patient overflow—the less severe cases—there. Critical cases are being airlifted to Vegas."

"Wallace approved that?"

"It was his idea," she replied. "He's got people working on a cover story."

"Industrial fire or something ought to do it."

She smiled. "The old standby." She took a sip from the mug she'd brought with her. "The hospitals will ask questions, of course, but we'll quash any investigations that may arise."

"All right," Harland said, pushing himself to his feet. "Sounds like you've got that under control." He extended his arms toward the ceiling, then knuckled his lower back. "I'm going to look around. Maybe I'll visit the infirmary. See how Ashdon's doing."

"You should get some sleep," she said, looking concerned. "You look like hell."

He glanced at the sofa, still warm with his body heat. "I've slept enough." He smiled wryly. "I must have gotten over two hours already. Besides, I've got to locate those kids. Dead or alive, they've got to be around here somewhere." He flopped onto the sofa and began pulling on his shoes. They were still damp, having dried little since their rescue from fire gear storage.

"They're *not* in the infirmary."

"Yeah," he said, "I know." She arched an eyebrow. "I told you. I want to check on Ashdon."

He ushered her out, following her into the hallway, and locking the door. *Can't make it too easy for the rats in our house, whoever they are.*

They parted ways at the elevators. Cynthia had business above ground, and Harland was going the other way. With the entire facility now awake, he had to wait for an elevator car going down. The car brimmed with passengers when it finally arrived. He shouldered his way in among the researchers and administrators. Many stared and a few smiled.

"Thank you," said a woman's voice, one he didn't recognize, as he disembarked.

He turned to regard the occupants but couldn't tell who had spoken. "Pardon?"

"Thank you," Marilyn said. "For helping Gilbert and me…and for whatever else you did last night to keep us safe."

The other occupants nodded, and a few clapped, as the doors started to close.

His cheeks warmed. "Just doing my job, but…you're welcome."

He regarded the closed doors a moment, then turned away, walking with a lighter step. He had meant what he had said. He'd just been doing his job, but it was nice to be appreciated.

He sighed. But, if he wanted to *keep* doing it, he needed to find those kids, and their snowy friend. He'd check on Ashdon first, though. Maybe get some answers to a few questions. Like what the kid had said to make the red bastard bounce him like a roadhouse drunk.

The infirmary buzzed with activity as medical personnel tended to the moaning wounded.

"Can I help you, Director?" asked a nurse as he entered. "Are you injured?"

He shook his head, scanning the faces of the nearest patients. "Where's Gary Ashdon?"

"Last one on the right," she replied, pointing. "He's still unconscious."

"Concussion?"

She shrugged, turning down the corners of her mouth, and moved along.

"Dixon," said a voice to his left as he strode between the beds, approaching Ashdon's sleeping form. "Hey, sir. When can I get out of here?"

"Kellerman?" Harland replied, stopping in his tracks. "What are you doing here?"

Kellerman pointed a hand at his bandaged shoulder. "Took one in the shoulder." He pointed at his legs. "And a couple in the legs." His nose wrinkled. "The goddamn stench…it was fucking awful…but I'm feeling *much* better now."

"Tough man."

"I think," Kellerman said, sitting taller, "I may be invincible."

The nurse Harland had just spoken to clucked as she passed. "Don't let him fool you," she said. "He's so pumped full of painkillers you could stab him with a fork and he probably wouldn't notice."

"I thought you ran out on us," Harland said. "You drive a gold Buick Wildcat, right?"

"Ran out?" Kellerman replied, sitting up. His eyes widened. "You mean deserted? No fucking way." He smacked at his bandaged legs and winced. "Does this look like I ran away?"

Harland barely heard him. *If Kellerman didn't run, who the hell was driving his car?* He thought of the shattered conference room door and missing kids.

"Easy, Kellerman," Harland said finally. He patted the agent's good shoulder. "I believe you."

"Damn right."

"I'm an asshole for doubting you." Harland inhaled deeply, exhaling in a rush. "Which makes it even harder to tell you that…your car's been stolen."

"Stolen?" said the agent. "You're kidding. By whom?"

"Sorry, Kellerman," Harland said, heading for the exit. "I've got to check on something…right now."

"But—" Kellerman sputtered.

Harland raced for the elevator. *It was the kids*, he thought. *The fucking kids stole Kellerman's car and escaped in it.* It was the only thing that made sense.

The girl's words on the surveillance tapes came back to him.

"Shivurr will save us," she'd said.

If they'd escaped, they must have had help to break the

bulletproof glass. *Could it have been him?* Harland couldn't be certain. There were other possibilities. For one, maybe the traitors that had helped Shivurr escape had done the same for Shivurr's friends.

Nah…it couldn't have been him, he thought, as he exited the elevator. *How could Shivurr have made it inside undetected, passing through the approaching horde of elementals?* It didn't seem possible. *Still…it doesn't hurt to check.* He'd put his mind at ease, then get some sleep. The vault had been sealed during the attack, so he had nothing to worry about. He was just being irrational. He was sure of it.

Nonetheless, Harland still felt a twist in his gut as he rushed across the floor of the archival vault.

He slipped and gave a shout, feeling his feet skim across the floor. He windmilled his arms, as his heart raced, but he managed to regain his balance.

What the—?

He looked down. A thin puddle of liquid, twenty feet wide, covered the floor.

He squatted and touched a finger to the fluid. He gave his fingertip a cautious sniff. Smelling nothing, he stood.

He rubbed his fingertips together. He felt no burning sensation, so whatever it was didn't appear to be acidic.

It was probably water, but he couldn't be certain. He sure wasn't going to taste it to find out.

He studied the ceiling, high overhead, but saw no sign of dripping water or other liquid. The fires had not made it this far (and would have been stopped by the sealed vault door even if they had), so the vault's fire suppression system had not been triggered.

He scratched his head, glancing toward the nearby freezers. *Leaking coolant?*

Shrugging, he moved on, and soon pulled open the doors to the freezer that held Winterboy's essence.

Empty. Just the tray remained.

Harland closed the doors. He grabbed the sides of his head, eyes wide.

All right, he thought as sweat dampened his forehead. *No problem.*

He took a deep breath. It was what he'd planned for…and now…whoever or whatever had taken the samples, whether Shivurr or the infiltrators that had helped him or someone else, Harland had them now. *But I didn't really believe it would happen.*

He looked down, catching a glint of light off the floor between his shoes. He stepped back and crouched. Another puddle of liquid, smaller than the last, pooled at his feet. *No, not one…two,* he thought, noticing a second pool of water. *Like footprints…left by a snowman.*

He thought of the spontaneous snowstorm that had arrived as Kellerman's car had fled into the desert. It was just the sort of sorcery that had earned the snowman his code name. Bigger than anything the Group had observed him do in the past, but it made a lot more sense than the fire elementals or the demon having summoned it. The evidence suggested only one probable conclusion. *Shivurr* was *here.*

Harland ran for the nearest phone.

"Get me a helicopter," he said into the mouthpiece. "Yes, right away…priority rush."

He hung up the phone. He'd have to notify Wallace, let him know what had happened. The good doctor would no doubt blow his top. Harland thought of the tracker he'd planted among the stolen bottles, and the handheld device in his office that could track its location. *He'll calm down when I tell him this could mean we're getting his favourite subject back.*

That could wait, though. He had more important things to do first, while waiting for his ride. Like get a lab tech down here to take some samples for analysis; figure out how Shivurr had done it. How he'd made it in, taken what he'd wanted, and made it out again undetected. *Like a ghost…or some kind of phantom of frost.*

Author's Note

Thanks for reading *Fire Demon Dawn*. I hope you enjoyed this side story to *Phantom Frost*, my first-in-series novel that tells of Shivurr's adventures after his flight from the Bodhi Institute.

Find out if Harland succeeds in his pursuit of Shivurr by visiting alfredwurr.com to get your copy of *Phantom Frost* (in eBook, paperback, audiobook), plus forthcoming novels in the series as they become available.

You can also subscribe to my newsletter while you're there, and be among the first to know about my new releases, special promotions, and extras.

Acknowledgements

Special thanks to my beta readers for taking the time to read the book and provide invaluable feedback.

Lorelei Pierce
David Kuik

Book cover by Damonza.com.
Editing by Clio Editing Services.

About the Author

An avid fan of science fiction and fantasy, be it in movies, books, video games, or RPGs, Alfred has also been, and in many cases continues to be, an Olympic freestyle wrestler (winning national and international championships), a computer scientist (M.Sc.), a software developer and consultant, and a video game developer.

He lives with his wife, Lorelei, in Canada, where staying frosty comes easy half the year.

Subscribe to Alfred's mailing list to get news, updates, and more at: alfredwurr.com/subscribe. You may also contact the author at: alfredwurr.com/contact-page.

Twitter: @alfredwurr
Facebook: www.facebook.com/alfredwurrauthor